P9-CEM-558

Praise for *The Tiger in the Grass*

"Some of the most enchanting prose around . . . *Tiger* connects the author's life and her fiction with veins as delicate and rewarding as traces of copper in an ore sample."   —*The Philadelphia Inquirer*

"In the same unflinching, unsentimental voice of *Stones for Ibarra*, Doerr sketches the facts of her life. . . . Just as in her best fiction she swiftly and effortlessly makes us care about her characters, here in her memoir we are equally enchanted."   —*The Boston Globe*

"Uncommonly elegant . . . Doerr's intimations explode in a seemingly placid landscape . . . her prose must be considered matchless."
     —*Newsday*

"Redolent of her beloved Mexico . . . Doerr casts her compassionate yet razor-sharp eye over situations with imbalances . . . detail[ing] the atrocities of village life . . . in the same lyrical prose with which she illuminates pockets of happiness."   —*Elle*

"Wise insights, couched in stunning metaphors and sensory imagery that lifts individual sentences off the page."   —*Publishers Weekly*

"Incandescent . . . written with great tenderness and understanding"
     —*Library Journal*

"Masterfully varied in its rhythms . . . Doerr's assured control of tone persuades us of her deep involvement with her material. She can . . . capture the whole sweep of a life in a single emotionally charged perception."
     —*Kirkus Reviews*

"Full of grace . . . her insights are like the stones of her stories, worn smooth by wind and weather. Through her experiences, stones speak."
     —*Detroit Free Press*

"Doerr is a master of selecting telling details and then weaving them together to create fictional portraits that have the clarity of photographs. . . . Her characters reverberate with truth as she celebrates the small miracles that, taken together, make up a life."   —*The San Diego Union Tribune*

PENGUIN BOOKS

THE TIGER IN THE GRASS

Born in Pasadena, California in 1910, Harriet
Doerr attended Smith College in 1927, but received her B.A. from Stanford University in
1977, where she was accepted into the Creative
Writing Program. She was a Stegner Fellow, re-
ceived the *Transatlantic Review* Henfield Foun-
dation Award and a grant from the National
Endowment for the Arts. Doerr's first novel,
Stones for Ibarra, won the 1985 National Book
Award for First Fiction, the Bay Area Book Re-
viewers Award, the Godal Medal of the Com-
monwealth Club of California, and the American
Academy of Arts and Letters Harold D. Vursell
Award. Her second novel, *Consider This, Señora*,
was a national bestseller. *The Tiger in the Grass* is
Doerr's first collection of stories and anecdotal
pieces.

PENGUIN BOOKS

Harriet Doerr

The Tiger
in the Grass

Stories and Other Inventions

PENGUIN BOOKS
Published by the Penguin Group
Penguin Books USA Inc., 375 Hudson Street, New York, New York 10014, U.S.A.
Penguin Books Ltd, 27 Wrights Lane, London W8 5TZ, England
Penguin Books Australia Ltd, Ringwood, Victoria, Australia
Penguin Books Canada Ltd, 10 Alcorn Avenue, Toronto, Ontario, Canada M4V 3B2
Penguin Books (N.Z.) Ltd, 182–190 Wairau Road, Auckland 10, New Zealand

Penguin Books Ltd, Registered Offices: Harmondsworth, Middlesex, England

First published in the United States of America by Viking Penguin,
a division of Penguin Books USA Inc. 1995
Published in Penguin Books 1996

1 3 5 7 9 10 8 6 4 2

Copyright © Harriet Doerr, 1995
All rights reserved

"Sun, Pure Air, and a View" (under the title "Consider This, Señora") first appeared in *Atlantic Monthly*; "Way Stations" and "Edie: A Life" in *Epoch*; "Low Tide at Four" in *Ladies' Home Journal*; "Like Heaven" in *Los Angeles Times Magazine*; and "A Sleeve of Rain" (as "Houses") in *The Writer on Her Work, Volume II: New Essays in New Territory*, edited by Janet Sternberg, W. W. Norton & Company. "The Local Train," "Way Stations," "Saint's Day," and "Like Heaven" were published in the author's collection, *Under an Aztec Sun*, Yolla Bolly Press.

PUBLISHER'S NOTE
Some of the selections in this book are works of fiction. Names, characters, places, and incidents either are the product of the author's imagination or are used fictitiously, and any resemblance to actual persons, living or dead, events, or locales is entirely coincidental.

THE LIBRARY OF CONGRESS HAS CATALOGUED THE HARDCOVER AS FOLLOWS:
Doerr, Harriet.
The tiger in the grass: stories and other inventions/by Harriet Doerr.
p.   cm.
ISBN 0-670-86471-4 (hc.)
ISBN 0 14 02.5148 0 (pbk.)
I. Title.
PS3554.O36T54   1995
813'.54—dc20   95–32391

Printed in the United States of America
Set in Simoncini Garamond
Designed by Kathryn Parise

Except in the United States of America, this book is sold subject to the condition that it shall not, by way of trade or otherwise, be lent, re-sold, hired out, or otherwise circulated without the publisher's prior consent in any form of binding or cover other than that in which it is published and without a similar condition including this condition being imposed on the subsequent purchaser.

For

(in order of appearance)

❧

Clive Miller

John L'Heureux

and

Cork Smith

Contents

Part I

The Tiger
in the Grass

The Tiger in the Grass

Yesterday was my eighty-fifth birthday, and my son, who has had lung and brain cancer for two years, gave me a toy stuffed tiger as a reminder to write, without further delay, a short account of my long life. My daughter, substituting a baked Alaska for a cake, whipped egg whites for twenty minutes by hand to produce a confection that towered on the plate and melted into a sort of heaven on our spoons. This backward look is for them.

It was only four years ago that I realized I was making my way through the thickets of life together with a scarcely visible, four-footed companion, who matched his steps to mine.

I first learned of the tiger in the examining room of my glaucoma doctor.

Sitting in a black revolving chair, my chin in a rest, my forehead against a strap, and facing an intense light about to be focused on my inner eye, while the doctor at his illuminated glass counter made entries on my record, I turned pessimistic.

"Let us hope," I said, "that I don't lose more sight in my right eye," and went on, "since I have only peripheral vision in my left."

Without turning from my folder, the doctor said, "Don't belittle peripheral vision. That's how we see the tiger in the grass."

Then he added, "It's also how the tiger sees us."

In this way, at the eye clinic, almost at the end of my life, I met and recognized the tiger that was mine and had been from the start.

If I began at the very beginning, I would probably tell you, dishonestly, that I remember taking my first reeling steps on garden paths while wearing rompers and ankle-high brown button shoes. Or I might say I remember taking baby chickens with me down the slide when I was two or three.

But how much of all this is remembered, how much absorbed

from torn and faded Kodak pictures, taken by my father, who died when I was eleven?

Unsupported by snapshots is my recollection of the time when, at the age of eight, I wept at the blackboard in French class. I still have total recollection of the event, but none at all of its cause. Was it simply not knowing the idiom, or needing to go to the bathroom? Was it fear of the teacher, who had snapping black eyes and wore two strands of jet beads? Or was it because the year was 1918 and the war had lifted my family from southern California and set us down hundreds of miles north of the house where I was born?

This was a place I had come to know intimately by sight and sound, touch and smell, a place whose arrangement of roof, walls, and intervening spaces I loved with a passion that occasionally flames even now. Did I weep that day for the door knocker, a twisted metal ring? Or for the umbrella stand in the shape of a copper frog with four holes in its back?

Or were my tears merely a child's acknowledgment of the times of band music and parades, of images of soldiers bleeding on stretchers or caught in barbed wire? Or of the spiked helmets and starving Belgian children in the posters people hung in their front halls?

Toward the end of the war, Spanish influenza crossed the Atlantic, then North America, finally to reach California. On certain days, decreed, we supposed, by President Woodrow Wilson's doctor, we had to wear white gauze masks to school.

However, on the day of my shame at the blackboard, I was unmasked when I cried.

I think occasionally of these unexplained, long-ago tears and wish I could cry them now.

After the war I lived at home, as before, with two parents, three sisters, and two brothers in a shingle-roofed, brown-shingled house that had been built with no sleeping porches and before long had three.

Bamboo grew along the driveway, eucalyptus over the tool-shed, and, at the bottom of our hill, three peach trees blossomed pink in a field that turned yellow with wild mustard in the spring. There was also a steep canyon, which every summer hid its rough slopes under green drifts of poison oak.

If it is evil to care too much for things that have neither mind nor heart, then I am evil. For in the house where I was born, I cared about the tiles around the fireplace, the oak banister broad enough to slide down, even the dumbwaiter, which carried up the trays for those of us in bed with measles, whooping cough, chicken pox, or mumps.

Once, two male cousins, aged eight and nine, sat on top of the dumbwaiter and tried to lower themselves, hand over hand, by its ropes, from upstairs to downstairs, and became stuck between floors. "Let them hang there," one uncle said. "They can cool their heels," another shouted down the shaft.

And so it was during all my childhood I touched such things as glass doorknobs, the carved border of a table, the inside of a windowpane when it rained. Outdoors I touched leaves, branches, and stones and still do.

> *Not long ago, in conversation, my son suddenly said, out of context, "I don't know much about this business of dying." As he might have said, "I don't know much about pruning this boxwood hedge," or "I never learned much Italian."*

Relatives lived three canyons beyond ours, in a bigger house on a bigger hill. They had room in their garden for cows, chickens, parrots, peacocks, and some captive deer. There was also a shallow lake, which rose and fell with the seasons. A leaking rowboat and some swans floated on its surface, and as children, it was entire joy, no matter how wet our feet, to row this boat as fast as possible in the direction of a swan and watch its flight.

On one side of the canyon in this garden stood a newly built Japanese house with paper walls. Sometimes we entered this empty replica through its wooden door, sat on the matted floor, and pretended to have tea from an empty black pot that stood on a low black table. After that, we sometimes put our fingers through the paper of the sliding doors. When the Japanese caretaker caught us at this, he would chase us away, shouting in his language as we fled. I suppose teasing and destroying are part of every child's nature, just as endless reasoning is part of an adult's, but if I could find the swans and the caretaker now, I would perform a deep Oriental bow of apology.

The elderly relatives who lived in the house ate chicken and eggs and drank milk from their garden and, I suppose, enjoyed the oranges, loquats, and figs from their trees as much as we, as children, did. Train tracks entered one side of the garden. But why? we wondered. Who got off and who got on and where did they go?

When we went, washed and combed, to call on these relatives in their house, we rang the doorbell and then guessed who would answer. It was bound to be McGilvray, the butler, John, the footman, or Alfonso, the valet. If we were lucky, it was Alfonso, a man who liked children, no matter how bad, who would lead us down a long hall to the room where the elderly relatives sat. They were an unusual pair. A divorce had made it possible for him to marry her. She had been a widow and wore mourning for her prior husband as long as she lived. She wore the wedding bands of both husbands on a finger of her left hand. She saw the world through very thick glasses and had a Brussels griffon for a pet. Her present husband, the male elderly relative, had a pocket watch that played a tune. He ignored his second wife's black dress, black hat and veil, ignored the second ring and the Brussels griffon. He saw her on the other side of the thick glasses.

Now they are buried together in a graceful, perfectly proportioned, circular structure, designed by John Russell Pope.

Floored and domed and columned in marble, it stands on grass among trees, not far from where we used to chase peacocks for a tail feather. It is called the mausoleum.

When Alfonso died twenty or thirty years ago, his will provided that flowers from him be laid on these relatives' graves. A dozen or so of us came on that green, sunny day and heard my oldest sister, Liz, say a few words about our Spanish friend, whose natural state of being was happiness.

I hope, and have left instructions, to have my ashes tossed, or spilled out, into the Pacific Ocean. As I understand it, California law allows the disposition of cremated remains wherever they cause no nuisance. So far, I myself have disposed of four people's ashes, three times illegally before the new law was passed. Each time the place was the concerned individual's choice, spoken or unspoken. Under oak trees, in the sea, Mexico.

I suppose I grew up like the rest of my contemporaries, on peaks of rapture and in pits of despair. I loved my piano lessons and even the hours of practicing they involved. How is it that all I have left of those twenty years are a nocturne, a few waltzes, and part of a sonata? Five people in my family played the piano, and, among them, I was the least accomplished. But I am glad now for every Czerny exercise I played, for the thousand repetitions of arpeggios and scales.

School, always a scene of heights and depths, reeled on, taking me from Latin verbs to Virgil, decimals to logarithms, and, in the case of boys, from imaginary encounters to the rejection of the awkward reality. Suddenly at seventeen I grew up, fell half in love, and went east to college.

Six weeks before I left for New England, I was invited to my first prizefight on my first date with the man, then nineteen, I eventually married.

This person, on a July evening of singular calm, took me to a championship bout. Part of a sell-out crowd of 35,000, we sat outdoors, three rows back from the ring, I in flowered chiffon and a wide-brimmed straw hat, whose ribbon fell in streamers down my back.

The moment we sat down, my escort said, "You'll have to take off that hat."

During the preliminary bouts, I learned a little about what to watch for and why it mattered. Then came the main event, a contest between two middleweights, Ace "Wildcat" Hudkins and Sergeant Sammy Baker. By the fourth round, blood poured from their noses, ears, and chins, reddening the referee's white shirt. I watched it spray into the air, along with one or two teeth. Ace Hudkins won the fight.

"Well, how did you like it?" my friend asked, as we drove home.

"I need to know more about the fine points," I told him, and, over a period of forty-four years, tried, without success, to find the grace and glory in this particular manly art.

The rest of our dates that summer were unexceptional, consisting of movies and long, aimless drives at night. We headed north, east, south, or west, making here a right turn, there a left, circling one, or two, or three blocks at a time, passing dark houses and closed stores, and sometimes coming back to start again.

This was territory we knew and, at the same time, could scarcely recognize. It hung in space between heaven and earth.

My son's first word was "car," and, as of two months ago, his doctor has forbidden him to drive. Now his car is parked outside his house and is visible from several windows. I have forgotten the details of the Chinese water torture we used to hear of, but it must be something like this.

I left California with a classmate named Jane, and some friends came to the train station to see us off. The nineteen-year-old who turned into the man I married was among them and brought with him three dozen long-stemmed red roses. These spent three days and nights in a container of water on the wall of our compartment. I sat on one of the green seats while the landscape disappeared behind me, watched the buds open and, twice a day, added water. Because of this attention, the red roses lasted all the way to Chicago.

"Those flowers!" said Jane.

On the way to Massachusetts, we stopped in New York long

enough for me to buy my first and last fur coat, full-length musk-rat, and to see *Good News, Rio Rita,* and *My Maryland.*

When I got to Smith, four special delivery letters from the donor of the roses were in my box, and Northampton was bright with fall. I signed up for music and astronomy and Catullus. Three weeks later, leaves began to drop from trees, afternoons turned cold, and, not far away and visible from my window, a boat started crisscrossing Paradise Pond, while its two-man crew dragged the lake for the body of a student, thought to have drowned herself there.

At this same window, looking in the opposite direction, I might see, a few months later, the mailman making his way toward me through the drifts of snow on Green Street, a letter from across the continent already in his hand.

With friends, I frequented a nighttime waffle shop, returning to my living quarters just before lockout. On weekends we patronized a pastry shop, where each of us ordered half a fudge sandwich. The result of these indulgences was going home for Christmas twenty pounds heavier than when I left.

"You look different," everyone said, and I was thankful for the straight, short dresses we wore in 1927.

That winter vacation, as far as I can see in my backward glance, was without flaw. Unflawed my unchanged bedroom with its window opening on a sleeping porch. Unchanged our old dog of mixed breed, Carlo, who lay on the chair decreed to be his, sleeping the end of his life away.

As though from a Christmas cornucopia spilled the scent of cedar, fir, juniper, and pine, the holly wreath on the front door, the garland on the stairs, the tree hung with tinsel, cranberries, and popcorn balls. The cornucopia poured out a gardenia corsage kept chilled in our icebox until the second it was pinned on the shoulder of a fringed, white-beaded dress. It rained down a dance and a new musical, *The Desert Song,* and some perfume named Nuit de Noël. It rained down a man, he of the four special delivery letters and the three dozen red roses.

By June, I had lost twenty pounds in Northampton and enrolled at Stanford, where I spent the next year and a half. Forty-seven years would pass before I graduated.

In the spring, when I was twenty and he was twenty-two and graduating from Stanford, the man who brought me the roses and I decided to get married in the fall. That summer I went to Europe with a friend named Lydia. Her father's first cousin was our chaperone. Her presence seemed normal in 1930. Of this trip, what I remember most frequently are the events following my purchase of a book. It was June, it was Florence, and the book was a Tauchnitz edition of *Lady Chatterley's Lover*, bought at a stall near the Ponte Vecchio. We were staying at a *pensione* on the Arno, and it was there I read D. H. Lawrence's novel, which was banned at that time and for the next twenty-nine years in the United States.

We traveled on to Venice, where Lydia borrowed the book, then on to Switzerland, where, in Zermatt, our chaperone asked to read it. When she finished it, three days later, she pronounced that the book must go at once. That afternoon we walked up a path beside a rushing stream in the shadow of the Matterhorn and followed it to a footbridge, where we stopped midway across the torrent. At this point the guardian of our itinerary and innocence took Lady Chatterley out of her bag.

Did she speak a few words? I only know the three of us watched together as the lovely, clear-printed volume was swept into the rapids and disappeared.

There followed, beginning a few months later, forty-two years of marriage, including two separate pieces of time which, recollected now, impress me as nearly perfect. Later on, after my husband's death, another came along, and it too approached perfection.

Totally spared by the passage of, not actual, but remembered time are the summers the four of us, as a family, spent at our first beach. These were the years of the thirties, when there was very little right in the rest of the world and everything right where we were. The town was small, well served by one grocery, one drugstore, a post office, and a telephone switchboard for calling out. Telegrams could be sent and received at the train station. I never discovered whether it was the slow economy or the fact that passengers in the cars that sped past on the highway never turned to look that prevented change. But I am convinced that the scattered houses on the beach and on the hill, the expanse of empty sand, the endless and untroubled coming on of days and nights, the slow hours passing unmeasured and unnoticed, were my first intimations of paradise.

As I recall it, the hill was wooded with eucalyptus and pine, with sage and buckwheat in the spaces between. There was a canyon full of honeysuckle, where someone had hung a rope swing from a tree branch. There was a narrow dirt lane lined with nasturtiums, another with morning glories. From the top of the hill, where we walked at sunset, we could see the ocean wrapping itself around the world.

On overcast days we drove to one of Junípero Serra's missions, where a Franciscan father in sandals and brown habit would point out Spanish and Indian relics in the museum. "The baptistery," he would say as we moved on, or "The organ," or "The chalice." Then all of us, unconnected as we were to churches, would listen with undiminished attention, even though this father had been our guide last time and had shown us these same things.

Then we would be let out of the church and into a walled garden so packed and crowded with fruit trees, vines, and flowers that a hoe, or even a spade, could scarcely find a space between the roots. There was a sundial in this garden, and a hollowed stone bowl for birds to bathe in. An elderly Franciscan was in charge of this modest square of glory, and, on our regular returns year after year, we grew to know him.

"It is beautiful," we would tell him, pointing out a poppy or a clove pink. "And you have done all this yourself." And the rope-girdled gardener would point out a sunflower grown from seed.

Then came the summer when, after visiting the chapel and the church, we stepped out into the walled garden and found him gone. A brown-haired, thin young man was in his place.

"Where is the other father who was here for so long?" I asked.

There followed a pause, and I went on, "Did he die?"

The new gardener shook his head, allowed a minute to pass, then said, "He was reassigned." With that he picked up a watering can and turned his back.

On the way home we discussed possible reasons for the transfer.

"He let the hose run overnight," one of us said.

"He forgot to fill the birdbath," said another.

But I knew another reason. They feared he might start to love this garden more than heaven.

A few months ago, my son, who must plan a future for his two rescued cats, visited the Humane Society shelter in the town where he lives. He investigated the cat quarters.

"How long do you keep them?" he asked the person in charge, and was told that every cat was either adopted or became a lifetime boarder.

"That's a pretty good place," said my son.

The second impossibly flawless piece, or pieces, of my life were the ones spent in various parts of Mexico. How is it, I think now, that I cannot find a familiar name anywhere on the map of Mexico without seeing, in the most brilliant colors, something that happened to me there twenty or thirty or forty years ago?

Once after a late-summer rainstorm we skidded off the road between Querétaro and Toluca, dropped a few feet into a field, completing two full turns as we went, and stopped at last in a pasture among a dozen cows. From the tree stump where he sat, a few yards away, the man in charge of these animals regarded us without comment or concern. A number of star-shaped white flowers sprang from the stony ground at his feet, like petals before a bride.

"This must happen to him every day," I said in the direction of my husband, who was already out of the car, examining the mud and the depth of the wheels in it, and saying, "We'll have to get a mule."

But almost immediately, the dilemma began to resolve itself, as dilemmas often do in Mexico. I recall no conversation. The cows' keeper, in his poncho the color of wet earth, simply raised one arm, and a small boy materialized from behind a clump of magueys. This child, happy to discover strangers and a car in trouble, ran off barefoot down the highway, to return ten minutes later sitting among coiled ropes on the back of the mule an old man was leading toward us.

During the towing operation that followed, I had time to see that, behind the meadow where we were mired, a thousand more of the white flowers shaped like stars had thrust up their stems everywhere—in the furrows of the field, in the ditch beside the road, between the broken boulders on the slope behind.

Then the car was back on the road, the meadow, mud, the cows, and white stars out of sight.

Once again on pavement and heading south, my husband, as though I had asked, said, "Those white wildflowers are called *estrellas de San Juan.*"

When we lived in Mexico City, we occupied one of two houses not far apart that had the same street number. We lived at Alpes 1010, and so, farther down the block, did someone else.

The mailman, considering this no problem, made few mistakes.

"Why not speak to someone in authority at the post office?" we asked him, and the *cartero* said, "That will not be necessary. I already know the people in both houses."

On Mailman's Day we gave our orderly-minded friend an extra bonus.

On the Day of the Garbage Man, ours came to the door dressed for Sunday, and so did the street sweeper on his holiday and on his the night watchman, whom we never saw by day. Each night, these guardians of our safety patrolled their assigned number of blocks, blowing at intervals, as they went, whistles of so plaintive a tone they might have been designed to mourn the death of a child in the family or a major natural disaster.

Carpenters and masons had their day, and construction workers in hard hats, who balanced on steel beams and marked their ascent with a wooden cross at each new level. This is a country where accidents are anticipated and frequently occur.

When I telephoned my son to ask, How do you feel, he said, "I am not one to say I feel well when I don't."

Instead of houses across our street in Mexico City, there was a *barranca,* whose steep slope, wooded with eucalyptus, fell abruptly to a drainage ditch at the bottom. People who had things to throw threw them here.

When our old dog, Bowser, died, Camilo Corona, the *mozo* who came with our house, suggested that we throw his body into the *barranca.*

I asked, possibly through tears, if he truly meant to dispose of a member of our family among rubbish that included grass cuttings and hedge clippings, rotting pineapples and broken bottles, rusty automobile parts and the skeletons of animals long since discarded there, and he nodded.

He said, "That is the easiest way, señora." Then he paused and added, "Where else?"

At that, I instructed the *mozo* to dig a grave at one corner of

our small square of lawn, and immediately drove to Sears Roe-
buck on Insurgentes Sur. Here I bought, not a shroud, but something else, which seemed to be Bowser's size, a heavy canvas
zipper bag.

Arrived at home, I saw that Camilo had dug a shallow hole.

"At least half a meter deeper," I told him.

Camilo's eyes were on the canvas bag. It was then I saw the
mozo considering my excesses in his mind. First, the probable
price of the canvas bag, then the mound of earth he had dug up
so far and the amount he had yet to dig, then the image of
Bowser himself, in death, as in life, plainly not a thoroughbred.

"The ground is damp," I told him, "and the afternoon is
cold," all the while knowing Camilo had four children at home,
and estimating the number of blankets the money spent on the
bag would buy, I still went on without hesitation. "The bag is
for the dog to be buried in."

Thus are our nightmares born.

After we had been in our house a month and Camilo had
settled into a routine of mopping the tile floors, washing the
windows, and sweeping the sidewalk, we began to notice that the
telephone usually rang, not for us, but for him. He would stand,
a short, somehow pathetic figure, with solemn eyes and stubbled
chin, near a table in the *sala,* his head bowed, with the instrument
at his ear, while he listened in silence to a voice speaking at length
at the other end. As for Camilo, he spoke only two words,

"Bueno" and *"Adiós."* When we inquired, after several weeks, about the caller, Camilo would always say, *"Mi tío."*

When we asked, "Is your uncle in difficulties?" Camilo would shake his head, look at the floor, and start to sweep.

One late-October day, Camilo approached us and, staring down at the mop and bucket, said, "There is illness in my family."

"Whose illness?" one of us said, and on hearing it was the *mozo*'s frail old mother, the other said, "We will lend you the money." Then a quantity of cash was handed to Camilo and an agreement made that this loan would be repaid out of his salary at the rate of ten pesos a week.

But the telephone calls continued, and after four or five of them, Camilo told us that his wife was in the hospital with an infection connected with childbirth. Again we lent money, again we established a loan, but this time we had to raise the *mozo*'s salary so that he could make the weekly payments.

Still the calls came, and each time the *mozo* hung up, we said, *"Su tío, otra vez?"* and Camilo answered, *"Sí."*

In November, Camilo told us there was an emergency connected with his oldest child. "She fell at school," he said, "and broke her arm in two places." She was at the children's clinic, he said, and partial payment was required.

"Where are these three institutions?" we asked.

Within two days, the *mozo* brought us the addresses, written in pencil on torn bits of paper. On Saturday morning we drove off with a map, the three addresses, and the legal names of the three patients. Camilo opened the garage door and looked solemnly after us as far as the corner where we turned.

Our first stop was at a stately old house, balconied, porched, and pillared, set in the center of a city block, hidden by a forest of trees and shrubs and the rampant vines that had been allowed to invade them.

"Maximilian and Carlota probably came here for dinner," I told my husband as he knocked at a wide, heavy door. A nun opened it, smiled, and called another nun. We produced our creased documents and inquired about Camilo's mother. The two nuns summoned a third. All three shook their heads.

"Yes, we take care of *las ancianas,*" one said.

"But this old woman is not among them," said another.

"We cannot help you," the third added, and all three smiled.

Nor had anyone at the women's hospital, our next stop, heard of the *mozo*'s wife, under either her maiden or her married name.

"We have never registered a patient with those names," the receptionist said, and turned back to her ledger.

"Do you still want to try the children's clinic?" my husband asked, as soon as we were outside, and I shook my head.

In the end, we did what we could. We raised Camilo's wages again, so that he could pay us back more quickly. But this time the agreement carried a condition.

"The *señora* and I have discussed this matter," my husband

said, "and agreed upon a condition of employment." He paused to look out the window at our sparse-berried pepper tree. "Your uncle must never call you here again." Camilo, staring down at the floor, nodded without lifting his head.

When we left Mexico at the end of our stay and had to catch an early train to the border, we gave Camilo a cash settlement to cover the required severance pay, as well as accrued vacation time. An acquaintance, learning of this, laughed. "Say goodbye to your money," this person told us. "Your *mozo* will be drinking it up for the next two months."

But at five o'clock in the morning, Camilo was there, sweeping the sidewalk, sober. He carried out suitcases. He gave us his key to the house. We said, *"Adiós,"* and shook his hand. When we looked back from the corner, he was waving.

If it is possible to remember too much, then in the case of Mexico, I do. Images spill over and threaten to become lost. But I know that I am better nourished now by images and echoes than I ever was by bread and wine.

Consider, then, my morning drive home from the American High School on my day for the car pool. Entering the district of Tacubaya, almost adjacent to the school, I would find myself in a slum and, driving through it, would often see three small torn boys waiting for a second-class bus. These were children who worked for coins at the supermarket where I shopped. Pushing and shoving their rivals, they crowded outside the automatic doors, waved their arms, and called out, "Me!"

"Yo! Yo! Yo!" the children shouted, leaning singly or in twos or threes into the customer's path. They fastened their urgent, sometimes infected, eyes on a prospect and called, *"Señora! Yo!"*

When I recognized these children on the street corner in Tacubaya, I sometimes offered them a ride to the market, and four or five of them would push their way in. Benjamin, who was eight years old and often helped me, was usually among them.

As soon as we started off, Benjamin asked me to turn on the radio. All leaned forward from their seats to listen to mariachi music and to the commercials that intervened.

One of these, much repeated on the airways and on marketplace loudspeakers, advertised laundry soap. A woman's voice would sing to us about the qualities of this soap. She would sing of its softness and its purity. It is like the white snow, she would sing, and my passengers would raise their voices too.

And now, with the car's windows closed against the cold, the smell of the children's unwashed bodies mingled with their choirboy voices lifted in praise of something they saw rarely and at a distance, on the tops of volcanos, snow.

When I write about Mexico, I transfer myself there wholly. I trip over its broken sidewalks, stop for freesias at its flower stalls, wave down its taxis. If there is time, I may still write about my Spanish lessons in a cold formal *sala,* where my teacher and I sat on stiff gilt chairs, with a tiny electric heater at our feet.

"I grew up on an *hacienda,*" my teacher said. "I had a horse named Betty. I watched the revolutionaries ride her away."

I may write about my rides on the thirty-*centavo* bus to the center of the city, where I got off at the corner of Madero and San Juan de Letrán. "If you want to see marijuana," people said, "it is growing among the weeds next to the sidewalk the entire length of San Juan de Letrán."

I may write about a picnic lunch on the island of Janitzio in the middle of Lake Pátzcuaro. We climbed on cobblestones up the steep hill and followed a lane high above the lake's edge to the house of an absent friend.

"Go in," he had said. "See the view. Old Juana, who looks after the house, will bring you a *refresco.*"

When we rang at the iron gate in the wall, we had a few seconds to look straight down at the named and unnamed shades of blue shifting on the water.

The gate creaked, and there was old Juana, barefoot and braided, clearly the product of centuries of unviolated Tarascan forebears. She showed us to a terraced table, brought beer, brushed away a fly, and watched us as we ate. The garden was edged on one side by the view of the lake, on the other by the abrupt slope behind. When we had peeled and eaten our orange and banana, we walked away from the lake, in case we had missed hillside flowers.

Then, with Juana at our side, we discovered, behind a high clump of calla lilies, a low grotto, lined with rocks, its dirt floor newly swept.

Old Juana smiled and pointed. In the grotto on the right

stood a pink-and-blue plaster statue of the Virgin, a candle burning at her feet. To her right, as tall as she, stood the figure of an Indian god, his bulging eyes leering, his square mouth exposing a beast's teeth, savage hands raised.

Old Juana's eyes were on us.

She wants a confirmation, I thought, and said, "The two together."

Soon after that, barefoot and happy, she took us to the gate.

The last of the happiest interludes that I hoard memories of came late, when I was a widow of sixty-five and, challenged by my son, went back to school to get my B.A. degree.

I earned the necessary credits in two places, Scripps College (near at hand) and Stanford University (far enough away to require my bed, desk, and bookcase to be moved). Even at the time, I suspected that I would have transferred my household gods, my *lares* and *penates,* anywhere on this planet, to any desert or jungle or Antarctic shore, to sit with these students, who, after the first shock, looked upon me as one of them.

This process could be quite brief. In one class, a student told me that at first she thought I was the professor's secretary's mother. My classmates commented in the margins of my stories. "Wonderful!" one student wrote of a phrase. "Ugh!" wrote another. "This should be a novella," from a third. "Cut pages 3, 4, and 7," advised yet another. "Harriet, try to use your own judgment," wrote the professor.

We believed we weren't asking for miracles. All we wanted was the perfect word in the perfect sentence that, when multiplied, would fill the pages of the perfect book.

A few of us, not including me, were published, and I sat next to them in awe.

I used to look at the faces of people crossing streets, waiting on benches for a bus, standing in lines at the box office, sitting beside me at a concert, and never found a person who appeared likely to read anything I wrote.

When I visited my son recently, among the books stacked on his bed were a novel by Ivy Compton-Burnett, mysteries by Agatha Christie and Cyril Hare, Listening to Prozac *and* Talking Back to Prozac, *the* Plays of Oscar Wilde, *Kipling's* Kim. *On a nearby shelf were some of his old books* —The Pied Piper of Hamelin, Dr. Dolittle, Treasure Island, The Wind in the Willows, Gone Is Gone, Junket Is Nice.

What things are there left for me to tell?

I think about the day I went back to school in 1975. Arriving at my classroom fifteen minutes late and finding the door closed, I stood outside it, holding my book bag and a note from the registrar, while terror assailed me. How could I, sixty-five and graying, invade the province of students young enough to be my grandchildren? Go back to the registrar, my common sense told me. Go out to the parking lot. Go home.

At that moment I remembered the words of Bob Gibson, who gained renown pitching for the St. Louis Cardinals. According to a sportswriter, Bob Gibson, in his prime, said, "I don't believe in standing around on the mound waiting for the catcher's signal and trying to scare the batter. My philosophy is, just hum it in there, baby, and let's see who's best, them or me."

Then I pushed the door open, entered the room, and the professor—for the class was Intermediate Spanish—said, *"Buenos días, señora."* And I knew I was safe.

I think of the people who worked with me in my house and garden. Hatsu Tamura, Setsuyo Doi, Hajime Doi. American citizens all, they spent the years of World War II in concentration, or detention, camps.

I asked Mr. Hajime Doi, who helped me grow flowers for twenty-five years, what his camp was like. It was in Gila Bend, Arizona, he told me. "Very hot there," said Mr. Doi. One hundred twenty degrees inside his house, he said. Therefore he dug a basement, so that his wife could sit there and keep cool. Smiling, he said that this project caused him to contract mountain fever, from which he recovered after two months in a hospital.

Then he raised one hand and smiled. "But," said Mr. Doi,

and, repeating the word "But," went on to tell me there was a stand of cottonwoods near the headquarters of the camp. When night fell, the men of the Japanese families went to these trees and broke off branches, which they planted in the ground around their houses.

Mr. Doi, a small, wiry man, lifted his hand again and smiled. "We poured water on these branches and they grew," he said, still smiling. "And by the time we left," he went on, "there was shade, shade everywhere."

And at that moment I wanted to apologize and bow a formal bow to Mr. Hajime Doi, as I wished I had bowed to the caretaker of the Japanese house seventy-five years ago.

I think of a conference in Park City, Utah, where I spoke one afternoon to a number of published and unpublished writers. I explained my late start as an author after forty-two years of writing "housewife" on my income tax form. These years without a profession, from 1930 to 1972, were also the years of my marriage. Hands were raised after my talk, and I answered questions. The final one was from a woman who assumed, incorrectly, these were decades of frustration. "And were you happy for those forty-two years?" she asked, and I couldn't believe the question. I asked her to repeat it, and she said again, "Were you happy for those forty-two years?"

It was then that I said, "I never heard of anyone being happy for forty-two years," and went on, "And would a person who was happy for forty-two years write a book?"

My son called to say he was dying. He had fallen down
and couldn't get up.

I think of what it is like to write stories. It is a completion.
It is discovering something you didn't know you'd lost. It is finding an answer to a question you never asked.

I think of all our children. Let us celebrate the light-haired,
the dark-haired, and the redheads, the tall ones and the short
ones, the black-eyed, brown-eyed, and blue-eyed, the straight
ones and the gay ones. Let us celebrate our vision, clear or
clouded, central or peripheral. Let us celebrate our uneasy foot-
hold on our shaken planet.

Now here is my fierce old companion, half threat, half friend.
If I listen, I can hear him breathe. I see him sidelong. Sidelong,
he sees me. We are still in step after all this time, my tiger in the
grass and I.

—April 9–May 18, 1995

Part II

First Work

1

The Flowering Stick

A Fable for Carmer Hadley

Once there was a far-off country ruled by a king who ordered his privy council to order the earls to order the mayors to order the constables to carry out the royal edicts. Thus the king was privileged to command his subjects as he pleased, by wisdom or by whim. But in all the realm there was only one who could turn dreams to substance, and that was the magician.

On the shortest day of the year, when dusk fell in midafternoon and the air was bitter with wind and snow, a beggar woman went to the magician's door and, after hesitating until her fingers froze, found courage to knock. When the magician came, she saw behind him logs burning on the hearth, a lamp lit, and brightly covered chairs as soft as newly shorn wool. She sat in one, with her bare feet on the rug and her hands stretched to the fire.

The magician said nothing, and at last the beggar woman spoke. "I have three wishes. Can you help me?" He asked what they were. When she described them, he said that, though he could make a fish walk and a tiger sing, the first two wishes were unattainable.

"The last one, though," he said, contemplating her. "The third wish, perhaps."

Then he opened a cupboard door, took out a crooked stick as long as a cripple's cane, and said, "Walk with this."

"I didn't ask for a stick," said the beggar woman.

The magician led her to the door in silence and watched her disappear among the hurrying passersby.

The beggar woman carried the stick for weeks and months. It did not fill her pockets with coins, or put an eiderdown on her cot, or crowd her larder with sweetmeats and fruit. So, finally, telling herself that she was not a cripple, she stopped walking with the stick. Hating to look at it, she took it outside her hut and left it leaning against the rough boards.

In a later season there came a restoring rain after an extended drought. Dust was washed from the oaks and cedars, pools filled, street gutters ran with the sound of mountain streams. The dry wash flooded. Fields, lately despaired of, turned green.

After the last shower, the beggar woman walked out of her house and saw the stick. At the top, leaves were pushing out of the wood. Buds were beginning to swell along its length. She left it against the wall but examined it every day. When flowers came, she started to carry the stick again.

Amazed by this phenomenon, the townspeople approached her with alms, the baker gave her bread, the weaver a robe patterned in royal colors, blue, scarlet, gold. Her stick blossomed in perpetual springtime, lilacs crowding lilies, violets edging primroses.

One summer morning, not long after sunrise, the beggar woman went once more to the house of the magician. She knocked, and he answered.

"Look at my stick," said the beggar woman.

"Yes," said the magician.

2

Carnations

She reaches through her invisible shield and takes lamb chops from the freezer and a bag of fresh spinach from the lettuce drawer.

She once read an article about a baby born without resistance to even the mildest threat of infection. A speck of dust, a draft, a breath, could kill the child. He lived with his sterilized blocks and balls in a plastic tent. The gloved hands of doctors, nurses, and his mother entered through hidden openings in the transparent walls to examine, feed, clean, and hold him, aseptically. He was fourteen months old when the account was written.

Ann Randall lives in such a protective bubble, but not alone. She lives with herself. They no longer speak. She can't remember being shut away. Life, like a subway train, simply began to recede, taking the people she knew out of earshot. Either they have stopped listening or she has forgotten the words. In the case of Elliot, her husband, she is out of sight and sound. His eyes focus behind her and his voice is directed to one side. His arms do not reach through the unseen walls.

Now she hurriedly unwraps the chops and puts them in a pan to thaw. She runs cold water in the sink to cover the spinach. She picks up her bag and car keys in the hall, latches the door behind her, and runs down the steps. She will be late for the hairdresser. The image of Joseph, courteously containing his annoyance, rises before her. She has the last afternoon appointment. He will have to stay until six.

Backing out of the garage, she finds no reason or excuse for the delay. She has had either too much or not enough time.

In spite of the hour, she stops next to the mailbox, which is half buried in shrubbery near the sidewalk, and opens it without leaving the car. She puts a few envelopes and a magazine on the front seat. There are two bills, an announcement of a sale, a letter to Elliot from his brother, and a message to occupant. And one more envelope, unstamped. A large printed word, PRIVATE, has been cut out of some publication and pasted on. Below it is the smaller word "Mrs." She imagines that a neighbor's child has left

it for her. With her foot on the brake, she opens it and takes out
a single sheet of paper folded once.

> your husband has been cheating on you
> how do you like that you holy snob
> why don't you give it to him you know where
> a friend

All the words were clipped from newspapers or magazines
except "cheating" and "snob," which have been printed by hand,
in black ink.

The plastic bubble explodes. Part of Ann shifts gears and
directs the car toward the freeway. The other part of her observes
from a reasonable distance and sees that although something (a
fist?) has hit Ann in the chest, she is unable to double over because of the traffic. The observer notices an object that looks like
a knife protruding from Ann's chest. She thinks Ann is driving
competently. She is using her rearview mirror, she is signaling
for lane changes, she is moving into the fast lane, doing a steady
sixty-two. She has, without conscious volition, turned on the radio. It is Renaissance music. Ann is listening to a pavane played
by lute and viol. This is followed by lively rhythms, subsequently
identified by the announcer as a galliard. He says the instruments
played in this dance were cornets, crumhorns, racketts, recorders,
and a portative organ.

When Ann hears him again, he is enumerating notable events that occurred on this day, October 15, in years past. It is the day Oscar Wilde was born. It is the day that Mata Hari was executed by a French firing squad. On this day, says the announcer, Hermann Göring committed suicide.

At the parking lot, Ann pulls out the ticket to raise the striped barrier and sees by the clock that she is fifteen minutes late for her appointment.

"You are fifteen minutes late," says the girl behind the counter. She is someone new. She is made up like a Parisian cocotte, thinks Ann, or like Canio in *Pagliacci*.

"We couldn't reach you by phone," states the mouth of the mask. "Joseph hurt his back. We don't know how long he'll be away. We've given you to Robert."

After her hair is washed, she sits in Robert's chair, her bag at her side. Her distant self reflects on Robert's paunch, which has been induced by an unbroken chain of two-martini lunches.

"How about going for something different?" Robert says. "Remember, this is 1975."

Ann is afraid that if she argues he will look closer and perhaps see through her ribs and through her skull. He proceeds, using at random a hand dryer, a comb, scissors, and a curling iron.

Carlos is combing out a woman in the next chair. She is in her fifties, and her body is a tightly belted gray wool sack tied in the middle by a belt. Her sloping forehead gives her the profile of a Nefertiti who was born neither beautiful nor a queen.

"Carlos," she says. "How old are you, Carlos?"

Carlos says something to Robert in Spanish. Then he says, "Forty."

He is much younger, thinks Ann, who is forty-six. She imagines his baptism twenty-eight years ago in a small church, La Capilla del Espíritu Santo, a few miles out of Guadalajara. His godmother, wearing earrings shaped like hearts, holds him. His mother and father are short and proud. The priest expects to be paid with a turkey, for they have a farm.

Now the woman has asked Carlos the year of his birth. The answer makes him forty-three.

"Never mind, Carlos," she says. "Age doesn't matter. You're my kind. I can tell. Why don't we have dinner and talk? How about Saturday night?"

Carlos thinks for a moment. "I will commit the engagement," he says. "Do you have a BankAmericard?"

Everyone laughs. Ann's observer sees her laugh. She sees the knife make a quarter turn. At last, Robert finishes with her hair. In a voice that is a tape recording of her own voice, she asks if it will last.

"Hang it over the side of the bed when you make love," Robert tells her, and everyone laughs again.

She gets her sweater and goes back to leave a tip. Drawing the envelope from her bag with the wallet, she hastily fits it behind the last bill, tips Robert, and hears her recorded voice say, "Thank you."

"Now go out and use it. Get it mussed up," Robert tells her.

Outside, she finds it is so late that traffic has thinned. In the sky, night has overtaken twilight, and cars have their lights on. Ann estimates that she will be home in thirty minutes.

She is less than a mile from her exit when she sees ahead, where the freeway bends, a figure waving a flashlight. As she approaches, she notices that the man has had no choice but to stand in the narrow space between the traffic lane and the chainlink fence which bounds it. There is an urgency in his effort to flag her down. She glances at him as she circles past. He is so majestically tall and black that he could be Chamberlain or Jabbar. Her off-ramp is just beyond. She accelerates, and moves to the right as she rounds the curve, and immediately hits a car which is stopped in her lane, hood up, warning lights flashing.

She wakes at midnight in a hospital room. Her second self, the observer, has joined her. They are one. There is no one to review objectively the pain in her chest or her head. Her left arm is in a cast. A nurse is holding her other wrist. She shows Ann some flowers on the bed table.

"Your husband brought them earlier." She releases Ann's wrist. Now she wants her to swallow a pill. "The duty nurse asked him to take the wallet from your bag. We can't be responsible for valuables."

She leaves the room on silent white soles.

Ann closes her eyes. The knife does not turn. In the room's dim light she sees the flowers. Elliot has brought an arrangement of ferns and yesterday's white carnations in a brandy glass lined with foil and tied with a lace ribbon bow. She supposes it is the first one he saw at the gift shop near the elevator or the last one left out at closing time. The flowers seem intended for a graduate or someone bereaved. There is no card.

She becomes aware of a memory pushing up from the bottom of a secret sea, breaking off from the accrued strata, coral hard, lying there unmoved by tides. It fights its way to light and air. When it emerges it is full-dimensioned, whole.

It is the previous year, and the month is May. They are on the road from Nice to Genoa. Elliot is driving. She is the passenger. They have just crossed the border. The guidebook says that Ventimiglia is one of Italy's most important flower markets. Ann has never seen so many carnations. Fields of them rise to the hills on the left and slope to the sea on the right. They line the road that stretches ahead, and she has forgotten where they began. They are being gathered in straw baskets, clove pink, spice red, candy-striped pink and white, pink and red.

On both sides of the road, men and women sell them at stands. Dozens are tied together to make a single bunch, sometimes all one color, sometimes mixed.

Ann sees a man standing ahead of them on the right. He is importuning them with all the flowers his hands can hold. Ann supposes that their fragrance hangs about him like incense. He is hatless and wears sandals. They are about to pass him. She hasn't had time to say "Stop."

Then, in an impact as clear and sudden as the clash of cymbals, Ann's eyes meet the eyes of the vendor. Their smiles meet and fuse. The second is held in timeless suspension, like a raindrop on a spiderweb.

His arms, lifting the carnations like lanterns, are open in an encompassing embrace. They hold the terraced vineyards and the twisted pines, they hold the marble figures and the tapestried palace walls, the tile on hillside houses and the stone on Roman roads.

Long after they have left the vendor behind, Ann turns to Elliot. His lips are moving, and she supposes he is dividing liters of gasoline. She waits for a moment, then touches his arm. "Back there," she says, forgetting that her vagueness would annoy him. "Back there, we could have stopped. We could have bought flowers."

3

The Extinguishing of Great-Aunt Alice

Great-Aunt Alice broke her hip when she was eighty-two. Walking about her garden one summer night, she fell over a hose that had been left across a brick path. She lay there until morning with her cheek pressed against candytuft and her feet on a clump of white dianthus. Her thoughts, rising like star shells over the pain, were various. She remembered the girlhood excursion when her long poplin skirt caught in the spokes of her bicycle. She remembered when the chipped beak of her grandfather's grotto-blue parrot had clamped onto her finger until it bled. She remembered the gestation and delivery of Theodore, her son. And she earnestly hoped that she would be found when daylight came by her driver or her gardener and not by Theo.

During her three-week confinement to a hospital bed, the only family visits Great-Aunt Alice endured with grace were those of her great-niece, Elizabeth, then eleven years old. Elizabeth brought strange maps she had drawn of India, France, and Peru, striped with rivers, crocheted with mountains, shaded with forests, dotted with wheat, rice, and corn, red-circled with capitals, and all bounded by shores of a thousand parentheses. She brought recent school compositions, which might start, "When I give my dog, Old Moll, a bath she smells like seaweed," or "Things I hate: roller coasters, Brussels sprouts, The Phantom of the Opera." Great-Aunt Alice felt more akin to the second generation than to the intervening one. Her son, niece, and nephews tended to cloud issues. Elizabeth and Great-Aunt Alice shared the same crystal vision.

Through the open door of her hospital room, Great-Aunt Alice sometimes heard protracted weeping. It seemed chronic rather than acute, a way of life rather than a trauma. During the fifth night of her stay she woke in the dark to the sound of steady sobbing beyond the foot of her bed. Switching on the light, she saw a woman sitting in the visitor's upholstered armchair. Long strands of uncombed white hair fell over her shoulders, and she was naked. Great-Aunt Alice understood very little about senility, everything about eccentricity, and was not alarmed. She first rang for the nurse, then regarded her caller. The sunken red-rimmed eyes, the mouth half open in lament, the sagging lines of the body, shaped like a wrinkled winter pear, gradually took form as a painted image.

She has struck a pose, Great-Aunt Alice thought, and wished for the reincarnated presence of Picasso or Matisse.

With her new artificial hip, Great-Aunt Alice regained much of her former mobility. She resumed attendance on Sunday mornings at her church. This was a modest ivy-covered stone structure in a decaying section of the city. Here it was that she had gone to Sunday school. She recalled coloring and cutting out pictures of David and Goliath, and of the baby Moses lying swaddled in his craft among the reeds.

Great-Aunt Alice, an inveterate nonbeliever, went to church because she always had, just as she took off her glasses when men were present, and called her car the machine. At an Easter service, she suffered a severe muscle spasm at the beginning of the Apostles' Creed. Feeling sharp pain, she rose at once, tall and erect as always, to tower over the lilies at the altar and the bowed heads of the congregation until she felt she could walk unassisted and without a limp.

Soon after the hip operation, Great-Aunt Alice became the victim of a series of small strokes. These were apt to cause temporary spells of what her doctor called disorientation. At the onset of one particularly trying lapse, when Bridget, her close friend and cook of forty years, was in Ireland for her sister's funeral, and Theo was away at a college reunion, Brooke, Elizabeth's mother, had to have Great-Aunt Alice admitted to a nursing home. Or, put more accurately, locked up.

The patient imagined that she was vacationing at a second-rate motel and, being naturally gregarious, soon had a dozen acquaintances among her fellow guests. One of these was an ash-blond widow, willowy to the point of emaciation and given to apologetic coughs. It was to her, one tedious afternoon, that Great-Aunt Alice said on impulse, "Let's go out to tea." Shortly after that, the two ladies exited through the empty kitchen, thus eluding their wardens.

Once on their own, they walked a few blocks until they reached the freshly sprinkled lawns and flower beds of a residential neighborhood. In the driveway ahead of them, a woman was backing her compact station wagon from the garage of a whitewashed bungalow.

"There's a taxi," exclaimed Great-Aunt Alice, hurrying on and signaling the driver with an urgent wave. She and her friend approached the car, now idling at the curb, opened the door to the back seat, and got in.

"To the Maryland Hotel, please," said Great-Aunt Alice. She had conjured out of a rainbow kaleidoscope of the fragmented past the site of her first dancing class and her first lemonade served on a palm-shaded terrace by a waiter wearing gloves. The Maryland Hotel, with its gilded chairs lining the paneled walls of the ballroom, its gold-and-crystal chandeliers, its polished floors, and Great-Aunt Alice herself in tucked dimity and high white buttoned shoes, were now of one flesh with thirty stories of concrete and black glass. That is, if Great-Aunt Alice, and her niece Brooke, Elizabeth's mother, and inevitably Elizabeth, were correct in their notion that nothing was ever lost. That the theaters they once played could produce on demand the voices of Maude Adams, Ethel Barrymore, and Harry Lauder, the boards of the great stages the faint tapping above the orchestra of Anna Pavlova dancing backward *aux pointes.* That the tree still held all the birds that ever sang there.

The driver of the station wagon wore thick, brown-rimmed glasses and a lime-green pantsuit. She had planted both feet on the ground when she was one and a half, and an aura of common sense hung about her like the aroma of wholesome food. Today she had realized at once that she must pilot the rudderless into safe waters, and set off with purpose and without surprise.

On arrival at the police station, she took the desk sergeant aside and hazarded a guess that her passengers were from one of several nearby institutions for the failing aged. The sergeant picked up the telephone.

Meanwhile Great-Aunt Alice and her friend had been served coffee by a pair of young policemen, and the four sat together, two chairs having been drawn up to face the bench next to the wall. Great-Aunt Alice, assuming they were midshipmen, immediately began an account of the June prom at Annapolis in 1901. After their second cup of coffee and some packaged Nabiscos from a vending machine, the sergeant interrupted to report that a car was waiting to take them home, and the ladies entered a black-and-white automobile whose revolving red lights and siren were temporarily stilled.

The nursing home, when finally hunted down by the police sergeant, had called Theo's apartment and found him there, returned prematurely from his alma mater. He had made a thorough search of the anniversary classes and encountered only eight alumni of his year, all so altered by time and varying levels of despair that none recognized the others.

Theo, reached in time, was standing at the yellow stucco entrance of the nursing home to meet his mother when the police car drew up and discharged its two passengers. He still wore his straw reunion hat, a boater whose ribbon band bore in golden numerals the year of his graduation.

"Theo, dear," his mother said. "We've had a lark. So many young men, and such good manners. They wined and dined us." Then, aside, "I don't have my purse. Would you give the driver something?"

In a later, lucid period, Great-Aunt Alice, perhaps more perceptive than the family would acknowledge, filled out a Living Will, the instrument by which she expected to be discharged into eternity with a minimum of fuss, discomfort (as agony is often called), and the inept ministrations of Dr. Hilford, the family physician. The esteem in which he was originally held had been undermined long since by familiarity.

"Doctors should be strangers," Great-Aunt Alice always said. "The only common meeting ground should be the examining table."

From the Living Will she deleted clergyman, lawyer, and doctor as witnesses and wrote in driver, gardener, and hairdresser. Once this was executed, she sent a copy to Theo, who wished neither to antagonize nor to encourage her.

"Gee whiz, Mother," is all that he was known to have said. Theo had married late and been left a widower early. He remained alone, having sought in vain for a mate as considerate and self-effacing as Amy. For his first wife, fifteen years younger than he, had skidded in a dense fog off a coast road and died on the rocks below. Even now, thirty years later, he often said to himself, She might have chosen a different route.

Great-Aunt Alice's driver and gardener were a father and son named Joe. Big Joe, small and wiry, took care of the garden, and Little Joe, tall and muscular, drove Great-Aunt Alice about in her machine. When the car was not needed, Little Joe helped his father with the flower beds and ryegrass lawn, occasionally trying out inventions of his own. One of these was his rooting out of two eucalyptus stumps by means of a personally conceived mixture of explosives. The force of the ensuing blast flattened one wall of the toolshed, lifted its roof, and splintered the old water tank above it.

Big Joe and Little Joe were originally Portuguese, from the

Azores, and without demurral or curiosity signed the document at her request.

The hairdresser was Oliver, born in Cheapside, London. Great-Aunt Alice associated him, because of his address, his name, and his accent, with Shakespeare, Dickens, and a nurse she once had who called her Halice.

She had patronized his shop for years. When she suffered her penultimate stroke and could hear and see but not speak, Little Joe delivered her weekly, by car and wheelchair, to Oliver's mirrored booth. Here he brewed and shared a heady concoction of frivolity, fantasy, and unswerving friendship. Great-Aunt Alice had concluded that in time of need Oliver would be of more use to her than oxygen.

Later on, this proved to be the case. When Great-Aunt Alice was at last brought low, not to rise again, Oliver went to the room where she lay, unconnected to any life-prolonging apparatus. Three pillows were behind her, and her eyes were closed. Oliver opened his black case, took out a brush and comb, and arranged her hair. After that, he stepped back to survey her.

" 'Igh style's your style," he said loudly, in the event that she could hear. And yes, he detected the remote beginning of a smile. Or believed he did.

Two weeks after Great-Aunt Alice died, Theo found a note in her bed table drawer. It must have been written on various occasions, months ago. The separate lines, penned and penciled, slanted independently across the page. For a moment, he thought it was a verse, unpunctuated.

Theo, it was headed.

> *Your father's Mesopotamian journal might*
> *Perhaps the piano tuner should*
> *The Helen Traubel roses need*
> *I had hoped*

Part III

Mexico

1

The Seasons

Yellow is the color of fall. The cottonwoods burn with it, and only flowers that are yellow go on blooming. At the edges of fields, against unmortared stone boundaries, in roadside ditches, grow all the wild daisies in the world. They are gathered in armloads and carried in sheaves on the backs of burros to the cemetery, where each grave is a raised mound of stone and rubble. The burial place, bare of grass or trees, is contained within its crumbling adobe walls on the fringe of the village—perhaps because the soil discourages digging—and is known as the pantheon. In this way station to heaven are honored the spinster aunt who had to beg, the father and son who died five years apart of cirrhosis, the twelve-year-old boy who jumped high enough to swing on a high-tension wire.

On the November evening of All Souls' Day, the flowers are lavished on the dead. By midnight, the barren holy ground, where children play by day with bone fragments, is drowned in yellow. Lit by an extravagance of candles in front of the crosses, the daisies almost grow again. They cover the names: Salvador, José, Rosita, Panchito, Paz.

Sometimes in winter, but rarely, snow falls. It forms an un-likely icing on the tops of adobe walls and red clay pots. It piles up on the branches of pepper trees and freezes the geraniums. Icicles hang from the corrugations of the roof. The *magueys*, usu-ally wreathed in shirts and dresses hung out to dry, now shine with snow like any pine or fir. Only a few remember the last time. Don Bernardino, who grew up on an *hacienda* before the revolution and can't read or write, says it was forty years ago. He says, "There was ice an inch thick in the water bucket. My pinto calf died." Then he forgets the phenomenon at hand, the blanched fields, the capped mountaintops, and says, "As soon as we were twelve, we went with the men into the fields. We worked from sunrise to sunset, fourteen hours in summer. They paid us in lard and beans."

The three plum trees flower in February, when it is sometimes winter and sometimes spring. Their knotted branches support profusions of white. "They are like wedding veils," says Angela, who never married. If it turns cold, the blossoms may freeze before the buds set. If one night's wind rattles the roof and shrieks at the door, by next morning the shriveling petals will lie in a thick mat on the ground.

These winds rush up the canyons and tear branches from the trees. They snatch off sombreros and the cardboard that covers the chicken shed. Concha, who will complete her seventy-fifth year in April, is crouched in the sun against the peeling wall of the post office. She watches a half-smoked cigarette blow over the cobbles to her feet. She lights it with a wax match from the box in her apron pocket.

Sucking in the smoke before the wind takes it, she regards the plaza where unnamed dogs skirmish among the drooping callas. Leaves and scraps of paper have been caught up in a whirlwind of dust and carried over walks and cement benches to the door of the church, where they are deposited just as the parish priest comes out. His habit is lifted by a gust, disclosing brown gabardine trousers. He makes for the post office and notices Concha, who rises with difficulty from her shelter to kiss his hand.

Summer comes suddenly, and all the desert turns oasis. Every afternoon cumulus clouds pile up over the mountains. The apocalyptic sky is referred to as pretty. "How pretty," says the storekeeper, who pastures three cows in an arid field on the outskirts of town. "How pretty," says the carpenter's wife, dragging a tin tub to catch the possible runoff from the roof.

When there is a storm, the thunder rolls up the mountain and down the cobbled street. It stifles the backfire of the passing truck and silences the church bell ringing for vespers. It mutters imprecations in the distance. The lightning forks into an ash tree, into the windmill tower, and finally into the transformer, causing a power failure that may last all night. In the flash there is a second's eternity of total exposure, the plow left in the furrow, the dented pot on the fire, the woman's face in the cracked mirror.

The cloudburst that follows drenches the chickens and the cats. It drips through holes in roofs to muddy the dirt floors. It carries excrement to the arroyo, which is now in flood. It pours from the varied terrain of the hills in torrents and rivulets. It sweeps across open spaces in curtains of shifting density.

When it is over, the obstinate ground yields to unsuspected seeds. Patches of short-stemmed flowers appear among the stones like colored lace. The air smells of wet clay and washed leaves. Children splash in pools and puddles. Some are barefoot, some wading in shoes. One little girl is soaking her turquoise-blue pumps. She has abandoned herself to laughter and doesn't see the puppy shivering on the step. Or the damp red bird in its wooden cage on the wall. Or the first faint green spreading down the slopes to arrive at last at her own house, where her mother is saying, "What a miracle!" And her father, "Now we'll have *chiles*. Now we'll have corn." He will buy her an ice cream stick to eat standing in her wet blue shoes.

2

Sun, Pure Air, and a View

One summer, a few years ago, a widow named Morgan Sloane, barely past forty, mother of two, came to live among a dozen exiles in the Mexican town of Santa Felicia. The hill where the foreigners lived with their bridge tables, vegetable rows, and wide green view bordered the southern edge of town. An overgrown strip of park and a zoo of fifteen cages divided the slope from the houses of the poor, who crowded together on the outskirts of the city. On clear evenings, jukebox music and an occasional lion's roar rose on the still air and reached the expatriates' open windows.

The first time Morgan heard a lion, she asked Carlos about it.

"Where is that animal?"

"In the zoological garden," he said. "There are monkeys there also, and macaws. You will hear them all."

Carlos was the *mozo* who came with the house. He polished the floors, watered the roses and the limes, drove the car, and, when there were guests, put on a white jacket and served vodka and cuba libres. The moment he was out of the room, some woman would say, "So handsome," and another, "Those eyes."

Morgan spoke to him in abbreviated sentences of the Castilian Spanish she remembered from a summer in Seville twenty-two years ago.

"How many houses are there on the hill?" she asked soon after her arrival, and Carlos said, "Eight. They are owned four by North Americans, two by English, one by a French, and one by Danes."

"Why have these people come here?"

"Consider this, señora," Carlos said, and from the edge of the terrace where they stood, he embraced the landscape, drawing to him the municipality of Santa Felicia, the *presidencia,* the cathedral, and the zoo, as well as all the plowed and wooded world beyond. "Consider the sun, the pure air, and the view. Consider the tranquillity. These people have abandoned their other lives. Now they have this." He lifted his hand toward scenery in general.

Morgan listened while Carlos, in these words, described flight.

Like the other dwellers on the hill, Morgan, too, had fled. She had taken flight from the sheer weight of the events of the past year. These included a loss of patience with infidelities, a legal separation from her husband, and her widowhood a few months later, when, stricken without warning, he died.

"Your husband has given you this house," Carlos remarked on the day of her arrival, and she said, "Yes," without adding that this husband, or former husband, Ned, had left her everything he had. Whether by intention or by mistake, believing he had half a lifetime left to change his will, she might never know.

"And you will live here alone," said Carlos, "until your family comes to visit you."

Morgan said nothing. She chose not to mention her daughter or her son, children who still existed, but somewhere out of sight, lost at the center of their teeming causes, inhabiting communes, organizing marches, tossing away their pasts.

On her first night in Ned's Mexican house, Morgan shivered for an hour between sheets that had been folded damp, and wondered whose side of the bed this was, Ned's or a woman's. Awake in the white room, she had heard the rain stop and had walked barefoot to the window to push it open. A gust of wind blew in the smell of drenched earth and a shower of scattered drops. Below her, at the foot of the hill, lights glimmered. There was Santa Felicia, most of its citizens asleep at home, the rest huddled in portals to keep dry, wearing newspapers for capes and paper bags for hats.

Morgan turned back to her wide bed. Behind it hung a long red tapestry, and now, for the first time, she noticed the headboard. It was made of heavy pine, stained dark. Across it, carved in high relief, swam two mermaids, tails curled, breasts high.

Morgan adjusted quickly to the pace of life in her house on the hill. Each empty day was a prism to hang on a chain. Stretched out on a long chair under the shade of a plum tree, she watched Carlos at his work. His smooth, honey-colored fingers tied up vines or clipped grass with easy familiarity.

"You have had experience in gardens," she said.

"No, señora," said Carlos. "Ever since primary school, I've worked for my uncle, who is a potter." He looked up and attached his steady gaze to her face. "Until your husband employed me last year," he went on, "and gave me better pay."

And Morgan realized that his talent with plants was the result not of training but simply of instinct.

Another morning, while Morgan half sat, half lay in the garden, with a straw hat over her eyes, she asked, "Where do you live?" and Carlos pointed in the direction of a village on the back of the hill, where the slope was less steep. Later she visited this place, where a scatter of adobe huts appeared to have been spun off by a derelict plaza into fields and gullies and a stand of tall weeds.

Goya, the cook, also lived behind the hill. Like Carlos, she had come with the house. Morgan made one inspection and, after that, avoided the kitchen, where the gaunt, lined woman padded barefoot across the spotted floor. Goya's molting parrot, when not set free to roam the shelves, hung by its beak from the wires of its cage and set off showers of seed and feathers over platters of enchiladas and pots of refried beans.

The cook, like Carlos, had a thin curved nose and the same deep eyes.

"Is she your grandmother?" Morgan asked.

"No, my mother," Carlos said, and Morgan suppressed a gasp. So great a space of time between them, one so old and one so young. But the resemblance was there, the inheritance of fine bones, handed down through long generations of Tarascan Indians, whose land this state of Mexico once was.

With the mermaids at her head, Morgan woke every morning to a brilliant early sun and the sound of a girl singing. The high clear voice, which at first she confused with birdsong, came over the wall from the garden of the house next door.

Tracing its source, Morgan found that a side window of her bedroom overlooked an enclosed jungle of hibiscus and mock orange. In one corner a trumpet vine strangled a mimosa, in another a fig tree bent under a climbing rose.

"That is the house of the sick *inglesa*," Carlos told her. "The girl who sings is her maid, Lalia."

"She is very young for that work," said Morgan.

"She is fifteen," said Carlos. "She lives in my village."

The sick Englishwoman was Fliss McBride. Morgan found out her story from other neighbors on the hill. Soon after Fliss moved here, ten years ago, she contracted pneumonia. It was a simple case, followed by complete recovery, but from then on Fliss never left her bed.

When she was recuperating, the doctor had told her, "Sit in a chair tomorrow. Go downstairs Sunday. Spend some time outdoors," and finally, "You are well." But he had to give up in the end.

The people on the hill visited Fliss and brought her gifts, custards and sweets, and sometimes slips of plants for Lalia to press into the crowded earth. At Christmas they came with poinsettias and hand-knit throws, and hung tin stars and angels from her bedroom walls.

Morgan, a week after her arrival, noticing an excess of flowers in her garden, thinned them out and delivered a basketful by way of Carlos to her neighbor.

Fliss sent back a note. "You have turned my room into a bower. Come for tea some afternoon. Lalia will tell you when. I am not strong."

But, Morgan told herself, sequestered as she is, feeding as she does on gossip and desserts, she is bound to outlive us all.

Morgan had never seen anyone as happy as Lalia. Singing, she emptied dishwater on the scruff of grass behind Fliss's house. Singing, she rode home on the bus from the downtown market, carrying cheeses, melons, cooking oil, and kilos of sugar and rice in a basket she could barely lift. Scarcely breaking her song, she staggered down the steps of the bus, allowing the driver to pinch her as she passed.

Sometimes at night Morgan imagined she heard her *mozo*'s voice rising out of the tangle of stems in her neighbor's garden. From her window she would see a flicker of apron strings, and early the next morning she would hear song again.

Morgan saw that Carlos also was happy, but in a different way. He was a man content with himself. One day Lalia told her that other men respected Carlos for his customary even temper and occasional quick right fist. Women looked out from the doorways where they swept or sewed or, in the case of foreigners, from the windows of their imported cars as Carlos passed.

Morgan, too, noticed him. In the *sala* she abandoned the letter she was writing to watch as, wasting neither time nor motion, and in silence, he laid a fire. When he drove the car, she sat in front and saw him in clean Indian profile as he spoke.

"There is talk of improving the zoological garden," he would say. "The cages are too small. A number of animals have died." He would point. "Over there, señora, you will see the monkey's hut. It is a barbarity." Morgan, declining to become involved, consistently refused to look.

She spent hours of sunshine on a terrace chair, eyes closed, measuring her past, drawing blinds against the uncertain, looming future. Not far away, her neighbor, Fliss, also reclined flat on her back, facing south. So it was that day after day Morgan and the Englishwoman lay on separate sides of the wall in independent retrospection as the mornings of their lives slid by.

Every day Morgan imagined to herself the unrevealed places where her children might be. She had reached them with the greatest difficulty, one in New Mexico and one in Quebec, to tell them of their father's death. The telephone connections were bad. She had scarcely recognized their toneless voices.

"Tell me how you are," she had said, and they replied, "All right." But what else was there to say to the woman who had rejected their father only months before he died?

These children were Morgan's hourly torment. She tried and failed to invent futures for them. Meanwhile the girl Stevie and the boy Greg, both not long out of adolescence, remained in peril. Morgan longed to push them back into infancy, contain them again in cribs and strollers.

Day after day, she cultivated hatred against her dead husband, Ned, and daily failed to achieve it. At any moment of any hour she would have had him back if she could.

And she continued to watch Carlos as he bent over a

geranium or pot of mint with the grace of a man about to kiss a woman's hand.

Just as Lalia's singing was the first thing Morgan heard in the morning, the watchman's whistle was the last thing she heard at night. This watchman, a retired clerk, arrived among the foreigners' houses on the last bus each evening and left at daybreak by way of a path that dropped straight down the hillside from the Frenchman's pear trees to the zoo. The watchman's whistle was his only defense against trespassers and thieves. It had a lilting, uncertain tone, and he blew it once every hour in front of each house. Neither he nor his eight employers contemplated the purchase of another weapon. Even though the cooks and *mozos* returned to the village at night, leaving the foreigners—women, children, and the aged, and the tipsy—behind, the stone houses circled by stone walls were considered impregnable.

Of the houses on the hill above Santa Felicia, Morgan's had the heaviest iron gate. Her wall was higher than the others and was topped with a fiercer dazzle of broken glass. Even so, Morgan understood it was not too great a barrier for a determined man to climb.

Before long, Morgan's day fell into a routine. She woke to singing, breakfasted on mangos and sugared rolls, sat in contemplation on the terrace in the sun. At eleven o'clock Carlos drove her headlong down the road to the fruit and vegetable stalls, the bakery, and the post office. She herself chose the papaya, the fresh corn, the hard rolls, but at the post office she waited in the car. Cripples and deformed children sometimes approached her at these times, and she averted her eyes as she handed them coins.

It soon became clear to Carlos that the letters the señora addressed to her children all came back. He would push his way toward her down the post office steps through the ranks of incoming clients and seated beggars, and hand her letters marked "Unknown."

"Look, señora," he would say. "Another letter has been returned. Why not investigate the address?" And with the car in low gear, they would climb the hill in silence.

Morgan had lived in the house a month when she asked Carlos to hang her mirror, a long rectangle of glass framed in scalloped tin that had leaned in a corner since she came. In the bedroom, the *mozo,* instead of taking up the hammer and nail, paused in front of her chest of drawers. On it were two photographs, one of a light-haired freckled boy with so much trouble in his eyes he might have just learned that his dog was dead. The other was of a girl, also fair, who could have been any age— fourteen, sixteen, twenty—a blue-eyed girl on a swing, smiling.

"Let me show you the place to drive the nail," Morgan said.

Carlos continued to look at the pictures. "Are these your children, señora?"

"Yes. Stevie and Greg." And when he didn't recognize the nicknames, she gave the full ones.

"Stephanie," she said.

"Ah. Estefanía," Carlos said. And when he heard the name Gregory, he said, "Gregorio."

Morgan saw he had further questions. "Here is the hammer," she said quickly, and showed him the spot where the mirror was to hang.

Carlos pounded in the nail. "Your husband bought this glass," he said. "But it was never put in place."

Morgan felt relief. She was wrong, then, to have believed she had caught glimpses of Lalia there.

Carlos stood back. "Look. It is defective." He pointed to the top, where a wavy band ran across the glass. "Step in front of it, señora."

Morgan realized at once that this mirror had a magic glaze. It was true that the crown of her head dissolved and undulated, but from the forehead down, a woman entirely beautiful stared back at her. Out of a smooth young face a pair of Welsh-green eyes met hers, a wide mouth smiled. Years fell away. This was how she used to look. It had all come back.

The *mozo*'s face appeared in the glass at one side. From over her shoulder he cast his eagle's glance at her reflection. Leaning forward, he touched it where it blurred.

"The defect is only at the top," she said.

"Permit me, señora," said Carlos. "I have a friend in the alley behind the cathedral. His business is mirrors. He can cut you a perfect glass."

Morgan shook her head. "This one will do."

No sooner was the mirror hung than Morgan believed she saw a change in Carlos. He began to seek her out with questions. "Am I to repair the kitchen drain? Shall I set these two loose bricks?" Wherever she was, in the house, outside, he found work to do not far away. He often gazed at her so long she began to invent ways to deal with the remarks she imagined he was about to make.

The more Morgan looked in the mirror, the more the *mozo* looked at Morgan. Or so it clearly appeared to her.

Now it was September. Summer was ending, though tropical storms still regularly produced spectacles of light and sound against the evening sky. On the hillside, the leaves of cactus were beaded along their edge with magenta fruit, and small pale flowers embroidered the banks of ditches. In September Morgan gave Carlos seven invitations to deliver.

"For the people on the hill," she told him. "For next Friday."

On the Monday before the party, Morgan, with a straw hat over her face, lay motionless in a long chair on the terrace. A loud interior silence prevented her from hearing Carlos until he spoke directly above her. As far as she knew, he might have been standing there, looking down at her, for half an hour.

"Allow me a suggestion," he said. "If you invite your children by telegram, they can be here Friday and sleep, one in the small room upstairs and one on the sofa in the *sala*."

Morgan removed the hat from her face. Carlos was regarding her thoughtfully. A current generated behind the *mozo*'s eyes ran between her ribs with the speed of light.

She shook her head. "That is impossible," she said, and almost went on, The places where they live are unmarked. Their houses have no numbers. Their streets have no names.

At six o'clock Thursday, at the height of a tropical storm, Morgan's daughter arrived uninvited at the gate. She had come up the hill on the last bus, with the watchman.

Carlos recognized her immediately through the downpour. "You are the señora's daughter," he said. "Good evening, señorita."

"Hi," said Stevie.

Carlos looked for luggage, found only a backpack, and led this Estefanía to a chair in front of the fire. Then he took from her, as she removed them, garment by garment, a plastic poncho, a man's red vest, two long scarves, and a pair of boots of the sort that soldiers wear. The girl leaned toward the flame in a torn black sweater as tight as skin and a green skirt so long it had trailed in gutters, wet and dry. Hair fell to her shoulders and covered half her face. This was not the light hair of the picture in the bedroom. This hair was the color of frying oil that had been used too many times. It was the eyes Carlos recognized, bright blue jewels.

"Permit me to call your *mamá*," said the *mozo*.

When Morgan came into the *sala,* she looked only into those eyes. The hair, the feet, the broken nails, the ragged sweater, the unhappy skirt—these things she ignored. She talked to her daughter in trial phrases, tentatively. Neither asked a question of the other. Morgan did not say, "Oh, Stevie, where have you been? Oh, Stevie." Nor did the girl accuse her, saying, "What happened between you and Dad? Were there other women? Do you hate him now?"

"I'm taking the Saturday bus to Chiapas," Stevie said. Morgan did not ask why Chiapas, a thousand miles south of here. Mother and daughter skirted the pertinent issues of the heart and spoke of peripheral things: Santa Felicia, the house, the other people on the hill, the lush countryside with its brimming lakes and ponds.

"I'm going to give you my room," Morgan said. "It has a window that overlooks the town," and she asked Carlos to take Stevie's things to the large bedroom.

After dinner Stevie spoke again of Chiapas.

"I'm going there to see Greg." There followed an extended pause. Then Stevie said, "He's working in San Cristóbal."

The relief Morgan felt at these words was like a soft south wind blowing across frozen steppes. So he was somewhere after all. She saw him in San Cristóbal, still freckled, still seventeen.

"He sits on the sidewalk in Indian clothes," said Stevie, "and sells jewelry to tourists."

This was something Morgan could easily imagine, Greg on a steep street of the old colonial town. She saw him in native dress, the loose white pants and shirts, the white *sarape* with the cerise border, the flat sombrero with the braided ribbon band. An unreasonable content filled her.

On the day of the party, Stevie instead of Morgan drove with the *mozo* to the market.

"Today you can take my place," said Morgan, and stood at the gate to see them off. The car stopped almost as soon as it started, to pick up Lalia, who, singing, waited for the bus in front of the house next door. Then the three went on together, two who spoke only Spanish and one who spoke none.

That afternoon Stevie, dressed in a caftan of her mother's, washed all her clothes and spread them on the terrace, where they dried flat like poorly cut dresses of a paper doll.

"Seven-thirty," Morgan had reminded her daughter, but at

eight o'clock, long after the six Americans and the two English, the Frenchman and the Danes, had gathered in the *sala,* Stevie was still upstairs. Morgan invented things to say to the guests. My daughter is ill, you are not the sort of people that interest her, she washed her clothes and they're still wet. Instead, she asked Carlos to knock on Stevie's door.

Five minutes later the girl appeared, and suddenly the lights in the room burned brighter of their own accord. The guests turned. Morgan turned. Stevie came toward them.

At first Morgan thought she was seeing an apparition, one who had braided blue ribbons into her cornsilk hair. Where had all this come from? The narrow white skirt that hung straight to white-sandaled feet. The fitted top, cut so low it barely contained Stevie's high young breasts.

From the bedroom window of the house next door, Lalia reported the party to Fliss. The long windows of Morgan's *sala* revealed the guests moving about, and all through the moonlit evening there was activity on the terrace. The gentlemen, one at a time, took Stevie outside and, each according to the degree of his longing, kissed her.

Lalia described all this to Fliss, who lay against three pillows on the bed.

"That is the dress from the shop at the market. Those are the ribbons we found. The eyes and the ribbons, the same blue. Now Estefanía is outside with one of the American husbands," Lalia went on. "Now with the English. She is back in the *sala* again, standing next to her mother. Two beautiful women, one old, one young. Carlos is passing wine and pastries on a tray. He is serving Estefanía again and looking at her dress. The Danish gentleman has come up to lead her to the terrace. He is kissing her hands, her neck, her eyes. He loves her."

"How do you know that?" said Fliss.

Lalia made a correction. "He tells her he loves her."

"Go on," said Fliss.

The party ended at midnight. Half an hour later Morgan and her daughter, with a wall between them, lay in their beds, ringed about outside by the rainbow of splintered glass.

In an unfamiliar room, on an unaccustomed bed, Morgan waited for sleep. For an hour she listened to the night. Wind on the magnolia leaves, an owl, a frog, and once, from the zoo, the distant protest of the lion. She was still awake when Carlos entered the house. She heard the watchman's whistle and soon after that the *mozo*'s familiar footstep on the stairs. She held her breath in the silence that followed. Then the door of the large bedroom opened and closed. Morgan suffered a brief attack of lunacy. He has made a mistake, he has forgotten, he believes I am there in my bed.

Returned seconds later to sanity, she heard, in this order: Stevie's light cry of surprise, the *mozo*'s reassurance, laughter, silence, a gasp, laughter again, a long silence. The bedsprings creaked.

Stevie spoke. The carved mermaids knocked against the tapestried wall and knocked again.

Morgan covered her ears with pillows.

"How did you sleep?" they asked each other at breakfast.

"Perfectly," they both said.

They passed butter and spoke of the fine day. Stevie spooned honey onto her toast. "My bus leaves at two," she said.

"Carlos will drive you to meet it."

Sun slanted the length of the table. Morgan saw everything turn gold: the tangerines in a bowl, the toast, the honey, her daughter's hair and skin. Time telescoped. Stevie could have been eight years old, pristine, forgivable.

On the same wide panel of sunlight, Carlos entered the room from the terrace. His long shadow fell across the plates and cups as he greeted first mother, then daughter. The day was beginning without confusion, without tears, like any other.

"The señorita's bus will leave at two," Morgan told him.

Carlos immediately offered an invitation. "Then that will allow time for you to witness a mass in the most historic chapel of Santa Felicia. My family is sponsoring the service."

Morgan's silence extended so long he understood it to mean consent.

"In that case, señora, would you be kind enough to bring your camera? For a few pictures."

So it came about that at twelve o'clock Carlos drove mother and daughter to his infant's christening.

The chapel was pink and old and streaked by recent storms. Carlos led Morgan toward the small crowd gathered at its arched entrance. Stevie followed, saw Lalia, and waved. A woman, grown thick at the waist with bread and rice and pregnancies, stepped forward.

"My wife," said Carlos. He pointed to three small boys at her side. "My sons." They were grave replicas of Carlos, graduated in size.

Now here was Goya, wearing high-heeled pumps and a lace mantilla. A baby with skin the color of cambric tea was sucking its fist in the curve of her arm.

"Imagine it, señora," said Carlos. "This baptism and my mother's birthday all at one time." He gazed into the worn face of his parent. "She has completed forty-two years today."

My God, Morgan exclaimed in silence. That old woman and I are the same age.

After the mass, Morgan took pictures of mother and child, father and child, grandmother and child. Of the three sons and a street dog, which wandered into range by mistake.

"Now you," everyone said to her, and Stevie caught her mother holding the baby, with Carlos at her side.

"One of us all together," they finally demanded.

Morgan had to cross the street to include everyone. She focused her lens and waited while a hunchback begged from the christening party. Trucks and bicycles passed. As she lifted her camera, she was shoved from behind by a lottery ticket vendor. A sparrow of a child tugged at her skirt. Across the street, hands waved and faces smiled. Morgan believed she saw the lovely, hapless infant smile.

At the instant she pressed the shutter, a legless man seated on a child's wagon propelled himself into the foreground and was included in the group. Then a military van stopped in front of her, and she took quick, repeated shots of its brown and battered side until the film ran out.

Stevie's bus left three hours late. It was after five when Carlos drove Morgan up the hill. As they passed the zoo, she turned toward the cages. There was only time to see the aviary, where a few listless herons pecked at a water trough and molting macaws dropped their indigo and scarlet feathers on the dust.

But Carlos had news. "A new manager is coming to the zoological garden," he said. "A person of experience. A Swiss."

He turned to look at his employer, who only said, "Good," and kept her eyes on the road.

As they climbed the hill, Morgan observed the cloudless sky and for the first time was conscious of Mexican evening light, the clarity of insect, leaf, and pebble.

Carlos noticed it too. From the top of the grade he pointed down to the plaza of Santa Felicia and advised Morgan to examine the panorama from her room.

"Consider this, señora," he said. "On a day like today you

can tell from here what kind of ice cream the vendor is selling. You can see the banker's polished shoes and the blind man's patch. From as far away as your house you can watch the big hand move on the cathedral clock. You can count the coins that drop into the beggar's hand."

Accordingly, Morgan went directly upstairs. She dropped her camera on the mermaid bed, glanced without mercy into the tin-framed mirror, and, as Carlos had suggested, crossed to the window to consider the view.

3

The Local Train

"It was God's will," said Trinidad. "Otherwise I might have taken the Wednesday train or the Friday train from Libertad to Obregón. But Thursday was market day in Obregón, when I could buy flannel, buttons, and yarn at less cost. Because I was sixteen and foolish, señora, I was not ready for the baby I had been carrying for almost seven months."

Trinidad sat with Sara Everton under the widening shade of an ash tree, on a pine bench that was as upright as a church pew. The two women faced a walled garden, where limp vines and seared lilies drooped in the heat of the April afternoon.

The uncompromising sun still paralyzed the air and baked the earth, although its rays slanted almost horizontally from the west.

Dust from the road had powdered Trinidad's flat black slippers. She carried ten small eggs in a wire basket. When Sara asked the price, Trinidad said, "Whatever you wish to pay."

Sara Everton realized that the eggs were the product of hens who scratched a living from straw, weeds, and piles of trash, and paid slightly more than the amount asked for a dozen large ones in the city supermarket.

From the bench the two women looked over the adobe wall, past the plowed field, the dry arroyo, and the village, with its three church towers and two domes, and across the broad empty plain to the mesas that closed the eastern horizon.

Sara inquired about Trinidad's children.

"Señora, I have ten," her guest told her. "Three dead and seven living."

Unlike almost everyone else in Ibarra, Trinidad had not been born in this town. Only a year ago, she had come here to live with her sister. The two widows raised chickens and embroidered coarse cotton tablecloths in cross-stitch designs of harsh colors: heliotrope, hot pink, and saffron yellow. Trinidad's hair, which showed no gray and was still as thick as ever, was pulled straight back into a knot, her skin was smooth over high flat cheekbones, her unwavering glance was directed from eyes where wisdom had been acquired without loss of innocence.

"Was the infant of whom you speak the first of your children?" Sara asked.

"Yes, señora, the first of them all, and a son, and the only one among them who was to be granted a miracle."

A silence followed. The tree shadow edged out, like a pond spilling, over the parched soil.

Then Trinidad said, "I think you know the state of Michoacán, where I was born and lived all my life, in the village of Libertad, until I came here, to these dry hills, to be with my sister."

At these words Sara Everton saw the state of Michoacán rise like a mirage from the clods of the field before her. As in the finale of a silent movie, when there appears behind the credits a vision of improbable rewards: a humble cottage almost buried in roses or a wire cage from whose open door two doves soar out of sight—like these illusory heavens, there now floated up before her the image of wet green meadows, red furrows of fertile earth, steep slopes of extinct volcanos serrated from crater to ground with ledges of ripening corn, low white houses almost crushed by their tile roofs. She heard the rush of water in ditches and canals and was not surprised when a lake materialized, drowning the famished plots of land, the baseball field, the cemetery and the naves of the churches. Within an hour there would be rain that would silver the surface of the lake as well as the leaves of the eight olive trees that lined the road.

Sara cast off her trance. "Yes, I know Michoacán," she said, and asked Trinidad what had happened to her firstborn.

"The distance is so short, señora," Trinidad said, "just fifty kilometers from Libertad to Obregón. Only one hour by the local train, and it stops often on the way. I traveled alone because my husband was to meet me at the end of the line, in the market town where he had gone the day before to sell a calf. In that short distance, in that single hour, it happened."

Trinidad sat very still, her hands folded in her lap. "I thought the train would leave late, as usual, so I almost missed it. I had to run the last hundred meters, with the conductor waving from the step and the heads in the open windows leaning out to watch me, to see if the conductor would wait or not. I managed to pull myself up into the vestibule just as the train started to move. You know these trains, señora, only two second-class cars, one freight car, and the engine. I looked in both cars, and the wooden seats, each one intended for three people, seemed to be taken, and many of them by more than three passengers. So I was prepared to stand, no harm done, I thought, being young and strong, when the conductor showed me to the one place that was left, a seat on the aisle."

Now Trinidad went on without pausing. "Across from me was a family of seven, all eating tacos from the mother's string bag, except the baby, who was at her breast. In front of me near the window was an old man who fell asleep, and beside him an old woman who became ill from the motion and continuously coughed into her *rebozo*. Directly in front of me was a woman with a boy of three, who stood looking at me over the back of the seat. The woman bought him an orange crush and then another to keep him happy. When he started to whimper she spanked him, and the two orange crushes that had gone in and through him by then burst out below and ran in little streams onto my shoes from the seat where he stood.

"Next to me was a very quiet, very ugly girl. She had pale eyes with no lashes, and a long face. Perhaps she was quiet because she was ugly. She was with a man who sat next to the window. His mouth was twisted by a scar that slanted from his cheekbone to his chin. He was drunk and angry. I think he was trying to make the girl say yes, to admit something, but she only shook her head without speaking. Once he shook her shoulder hard enough to make her teeth rattle, and once he slapped her cheek so hard she cried. Twice the conductor came to warn this man, saying that he would put him off at the next stop if the disturbance continued. Then the man would look out the open window with his lips moving, one hand clenched to his knee and the other in his pocket, and we would have a moment's peace.

"But he always returned to the argument, angrier than before, until at last, when there were only ten minutes of the trip left, the girl spoke, still not looking at him. 'Then kill me,' she said. And when he heard these words, out of his pocket came his hand, holding a knife that looked as if it lived there. He switched it open and stabbed her in the chest, in the neck, in whatever part of her he encountered, while she struggled and screamed, until the conductor came running and, with the help of three young men who were passengers, disarmed this man and took him away, his arms bound to his sides with rope."

Now Trinidad looked at Sara. "And the plain girl, with her pale eyes wide open and blood pouring from her mouth like coffee from the pot, lay dead with her head on my shoulder and her blood running down to my knees, soaking through my shawl and my apron and my dress and my garments beneath. Soaking through my skin until it reached my unborn child and he swam in her blood.

"So great was my fright, señora, that I could not utter a word and no tears came. Two men carried off the girl, and when we arrived in Obregón a few minutes later, there stood my husband, fixed to the platform, thinking that the people from the train who helped me walk to him were bringing him an expiring wife.

"And so it was that my first son, Florencio, whom we call Lencho, was born five weeks before full term, and we feared he might bear some mark of the shock he and I had suffered. But, señora, he was a perfect baby, unmarked, unscarred. Only later we began to notice that when I dropped the cover of a pan, Lencho did not start and when I called to him by name he did not turn. So after a few months we realized that Lencho was deaf and a little later came to know that he couldn't talk.

"Then I gave birth to more children, a year and a half apart, and we continued to farm our small plot of land in Libertad.

Lencho was very intelligent. He watched our mouths and learned to understand some of the things we said. Of course, he could not go to school with the others. Instead, he helped his father plant corn and *chiles* in the spring, and every morning he took the cow to graze.

"And so nine years passed in that part of Michoacán, which is my *tierra,* my true home. One day my husband's cousin came, who had not been in Libertad since he left to study at preparatory school and college, and then the university, where he was trained to be a doctor. He looked at Lencho and made him open his mouth.

"Then he told me I must take the boy to a specialist in San Luis Potosi, which is five hundred kilometers north of Libertad. The cousin said to waste no time. So I borrowed the money for the bus fare, promising young chickens and fresh cow's milk in return. Two days after we arrived in San Luis the specialist operated on Lencho's throat. The surgery lasted three hours, and afterwards, when Lencho was in his bed again, as white and quiet as a corpse, I thought: They have brought him back to this room to die.

"But when he woke up an hour later he turned his head toward a step or a voice. He started making sounds, and in the next weeks and months the sounds became words."

Trinidad looked at the American woman. "Now I have told you how the Virgin protected Lencho," she said.

Sara nodded. She said, "Yes."

Trinidad, standing to leave in the gathering dusk, told Sara how soon after Lencho's cure the whole family traveled across two states of Mexico to thank the Virgin of San Juan de los Lagos, who is responsible for miracles of this sort. From the bus station they crossed to the church, where they waited for two hours in the courtyard, on their knees among the kneeling crowd, until it was their turn to enter. When they finally reached the altar, Trinidad lit a candle for Lencho to place among the hundreds already lighted there, and each child had a flower to add to the others that lay in heaps and sheaves at the Virgin's feet.

"She might have walked away on flowers, señora," said Trinidad.

By the time she went off with the empty egg basket, the shadow of the ash tree had climbed the eastern wall. Its branches scarcely stirred. The birds that inhabited it might already have settled in for the night.

Sara lingered there, staring across the darkening valley to the hills lying in full sun beyond. She closed her eyes and listened. For a few seconds no door slammed, no dog barked, no child called. It was so still she could hear the turn of a leaf, the fold of a wing.

4

Way Stations

The train from the border was two hours late, and when it finally rolled into the station, no one left the sleeping car.

"They missed it in Juárez," said Richard Everton.

"Or were left behind after one of the stops," said his wife, Sara. "In Palacios, or El Alamo, or Santa Luz. Maybe Steve wanted to take pictures." But her concern began to sound in her voice. "As for Kate," she went on, "Kate's lived in so many time zones that she's stopped needing clocks. She's like the people here," Sara said. "She tells time by the sun and the stars."

And once more the Evertons walked the length of the train,

from the locomotive to the rear car, making their way through crowds of laden passengers, boarding and unboarding the day coaches.

Richard was questioning the conductor when Sara called, "There's Kate," and waved to her friend, a reluctant, red-haired woman who clung to a furled umbrella and hesitated at the top of the train's rear steps as if the platform were thirty feet below and in flames.

Sara had time to say to Richard, "Something's wrong," before she lifted her face to Kate and asked, "Where's Steve?" For Kate had apparently come by herself to spend a week in Ibarra.

The Evertons stood with the porter below the vestibule, and all three raised an arm to bring Kate to them before she could suffer a change of heart and simply travel on.

At last she spoke. "I'm alone," she said, and stepped down.

The Evertons led their guest away from the station, saying nothing to each other and only "No" to the vendors of bananas and tacos, baskets and lace. Except that Kate, approached by a ragged child crusted with dust, bought his entire stock of candy-coated gum and paid for it in dollars.

While Richard lifted Kate's suitcases into the car, she stood motionless, her umbrella planted against the ground like a divining rod.

Richard took it from her. "There won't be rain for three months. Not until June," he said.

Sara, looking in the direction of the platform, said, "Here comes Inocencia."

An old woman, wrapped in a number of shawls and bent as a gnarled branch, approached them in a patchwork of skirts that swept the dirt and stirred up discarded trash.

Ancient of days, Sara thought, and of winds and frosts and cobblestones. "Inocencia begs in Ibarra," she explained to Kate, "and here in Concepción, when she can get a ride."

On the way back to Ibarra, Kate sat with Richard in front, and Sara behind with Inocencia. I would like to call her Chencha, as the *cura* does, thought Sara. It is less formal. But there was something in the old woman's blackbird eyes, something about her slippered feet set parallel on the floor, that discouraged intimacy.

They turned north from the station toward the mountains and in ten minutes were on a narrow road winding around hillsides and through gullies.

"How was the train?" Sara asked. "Did the fan work? Was there ice?"

As though she had not heard, Kate made no response. She has traveled so much that details like these are immaterial to her, Sara supposed.

Neither of the Evertons asked about Steve. Once Richard pointed to three silos clustered in the corner of a field like white wigwams and once to a vineyard covered with the green mist of breaking leaves. "Revisions in the landscape since you saw it last," he said.

From the back seat Sara watched Kate nod.

After that Richard said nothing at all and Sara spoke once. Reminded when they passed the chapel of a crumbling *hacienda*, she said, "Next Wednesday is the Day of the Priests. We are invited to a program." This information produced no answer.

Not until they turned west at a pond where cows grazed in the muddy bottom, not until the car started to climb toward the hills, did Kate utter a word. Then she said, "We are separated." Not "Steve and I." Simply "We." As if she were pronouncing separation to be a universal condition, a state in which every man and woman slept and woke. Sara looked at the back of Richard's head, as if for reassurance.

As they neared the summit of the mountain grade, Kate spoke again. "Steve decided at the border not to come. There was no way to let you know in time." She appeared to be talking to herself. "He says living with me is like serving a sentence." She might have been addressing the burro asleep on its feet in the road ahead of them.

But they blame themselves, Sara thought, in sight of each other, for the death of the child. Since the day of the accident, guilt has taken up quarters with them. And blame just outside the door, rattling the knob.

Divide the blame, Sara wanted to tell her friend, who sat mute and stiff in the seat ahead. Blame the precocious two-year-old

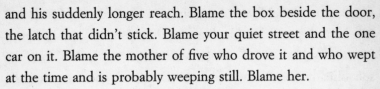

and his suddenly longer reach. Blame the box beside the door, the latch that didn't stick. Blame your quiet street and the one car on it. Blame the mother of five who drove it and who wept at the time and is probably weeping still. Blame her.

Sara said all these things silently to Kate as they reached the top of the grade. Now the car was bumping down the stony track into Ibarra, and Inocencia was edging forward from the back seat.

"She wants to get out here," Sara told Richard. "In front of the church." For these steps seemed a better source of alms than either the grocer's or the baker's door, now that a dozen black-shawled women and a few old men were gathering to celebrate noon mass.

Descending to the street with a rattle of coins, Inocencia stooped to search the ground as if she might discover a silver peso among the cobbles. Then she made her way around the car, approached Kate's window, and thrust in a hand like a parrot's claw.

Kate seemed not to recognize its purpose. Eventually Richard had to extend his long arm across her in order to drop small change into the old woman's palm.

"God will repay you," said Inocencia.

The beggar addressed this remark to everyone in the car. When, wondered the Evertons. How, wondered Kate.

For the first three days of her visit Kate came to breakfast at ten, two hours after Richard had left for the mine and Sara had gone into the early shade of the garden to water and trim. With the sun already above the trees, the Evertons' guest entered the whitewashed kitchen, found coffee, fruit, and rolls, and ate in front of the dining room window. Through it she gazed at Sara tearing apart iris and dividing ferns. And gazed farther to the olive trees and beyond them to the high wooden gate that opened on the road. Entering this gate every morning as Kate started to eat and advancing with deliberation toward the house came Lourdes the cook, who arrived in midmorning to prepare lunch and dinner and to save, if she could, the Evertons' souls.

Kate's Spanish was limited to simple phrases. Those of curiosity: "What is the destination of this bus?" or "Is there a direct route to the international airport?" And those of crisis: "Please deliver an urgent message," or "A single room, please. My husband is not with me." When Lourdes came into the dining room to talk, the visitor understood only a few words.

Kate knew the words for thin and eat, and also for when and why, but not the answers. She knew that Don Esteban was Steve. So when Lourdes said, "Will not your husband follow you by a later train?" and "Have you had an illness to make you look so pale?" Kate, rather than let an awkward silence fall, replied indiscriminately with *"No"* or *"Sí."*

Concerned by the portent of these responses, Lourdes began

to leave talismans among the guest's folded clothes. So that when Kate rummaged for a sweater or a scarf she would find bits of knotted twine or graying ribbon hidden among them. Once she discovered half a tortilla curling on her windowsill.

On the third day of her visit, as she lay apparently asleep in a hammock woven of maguey, she opened her eyes to ask Sara where the scraps she had found came from and what they meant.

"Lourdes wants you to be well and safe."

"I thought it might have something to do with getting into heaven."

"That too," said Sara.

The hammock had not known such constant use since the day, a month before, when Richard strung it up. Here, a few feet above the ground, Kate lay morning and afternoon, often with an arm across her eyes.

She can't sleep at night, Sara told herself, and abandoned hopes of conversation. Instead, she skirted the hammock at a distance and suppressed impulses to point out hummingbirds in the jasmine or a stray turkey on the path. Once or twice a day she was called to the gate by a visitor.

At these times Kate, roused from sleep or sorrow, would become aware of talk across the garden. "Señora," she would hear a strange voice say, and then Sara's *"Dígame."*

"What does that mean?" the guest finally asked. *"Dígame."*

"It means 'tell me.'"

🌀

That night in bed, Sara said to Richard, "Do you think that hammock lends itself to grieving?" and Richard said that if so, it was a problem easily cured.

He was almost asleep when Sara said, "Do you think she should take a trip somewhere? Arrive by riverboat and narrow-gauge railroad at a place she doesn't know?"

Richard said, "That might work."

"She used to be obsessed by going places," and Sara reminded him of Kate's years of impulsive wanderings.

"But you're not her Saint Christopher," said Richard.

He removed the hammock before breakfast the next morning.

"The cords were fraying," Richard later lied to Kate.

That afternoon the two women walked up the dirt lane to the ruined monastery of Tepozán. Next to the chapel, the monks' roofless habitations had become wells of sunlight. Kate and Sara crossed the paved courtyard to lean on the balustrade that bordered an arroyo. The place was ringed with silence. They heard neither the ore truck climbing the mountain nor the shouts of boys carrying hot lunches to the miners. Now and then an old woman on a cane limped into the chapel and another limped out.

"Do they still use the chapel for mass?" asked Kate.

"Only on special days." Sara turned her face up to the sun. "There's a procession once a year behind the effigy of *El Señor,* the patron of Tepozán."

"*Señor* who?"

"Christ," said Sara.

After a pause, Kate said, "Didn't we have a picnic under those trees?" surprising Sara, who was convinced by now that her friend had erased permanently any memories, even the slightly happy ones, of her past.

Sara remembered the picnic under the ash trees. It had been three years ago, a wet green August day between the rainstorms of one afternoon and the next. The Evertons had brought Kate and Steve to the monastery to eat because of this greenness, of the ash trees, of the corn planted in the patio behind, of the twisted grapevine near the wall, even of the cactus on this hill.

That day at Tepozán they had spread a wool *sarape* on the pink stone of the balustrade and sat along it in a row. Damp weeds made a tangled rug under their feet, and the washed leaves overhead still dripped from time to time. While they ate bread and cheese and slices of papaya, a herd of goats chewed their way across the hillside behind, shaking bells and loosening small rains of stones. The picnic was so tranquil, with the sun on their backs and the stillness held in suspension, that Sara believed a charm had fallen on each of them.

Then Steve said, "How is the experiment working out?"

At first the Evertons thought he was speaking of a medical experiment, of pills that might, in combination with others, add new dimensions to Richard's life.

"What experiment?" said Richard.

"The mine," said Steve. And again Richard and Sara were silent. For they had long ago stopped thinking of the mine operation as an experiment. The experiment had turned, almost from the beginning, into a lifelong effort.

"How much longer will you be here?" Steve asked, as if he considered the tunnels and ladders of the mine, the rough streets and leaning roofs of Ibarra, and the thousand people who lived under these roofs to be a point of interest in a travel guide, recommended for a side trip.

"Indefinitely," Richard said.

And now, three years later, standing with Kate at the monastery in hot dry March, Sara said, "That was the greenest day of the summer."

Kate said nothing. Finally she walked away, letting her words drift back over her shoulder.

"How can we live with death between us?"

That "we" again, thought Sara.

That night in bed, Sara said to Richard, "It's hopeless. She is numb to everything."

He turned to his wife. "Tell me what to do."

"You could show her the mine."

The following day Richard sent his foreman to the house in the pickup truck with instructions to bring Kate to the mine. She was gone all morning and returned at one, blown and dusty.

She found Sara on the porch, looking out over Ibarra as if she had noticed it today for the first time. Kate sat on a bench beside her.

"This is what Richard has always wanted, isn't it? This place, these people, you in this house." Then she went on as if in logical sequence, "I think Steve is in love with another woman. Someone happy."

Later she said, "All that machinery, those crushers and cells and belts. They're like Richard's personal creations."

Half metal and half hope, Sara silently commented. An alloy.

An hour later Kate said, as though there had been no pause, "Then he and the foreman drove me all over the hills to look down the shafts of abandoned mines."

Earlier, from the porch, Sara had noticed the pickup traveling cross-country, winding steeply into sight around one hillside and out of sight around another. So they had visited them all. Reciting the names of mines to herself, Sara strung them together like beads.

The Mercy, the Rattlesnake, the Incarnation, La Lulu.

On Tuesday the two women followed the eroded ruts that led from the house to the village. As they entered the plaza, a spiral of dust whirled from the arcade, lingered over the cobblestones to suck up straw and paper, then careened in their direction.

"It was cleaner three years ago," said Kate.

"You came in August, in the rainy season. Summer in Ibarra is a different time, in a different place."

They sat on a cement bench facing the church. The bench had been donated by Pepsi-Cola, whose name was lettered on the back.

"Steve and I should have been religious," said Kate.

"Why?"

"Religious people blame God."

Out of his house next to the church appeared the *cura,* followed by his elderly assistant. As soon as the priests reached the street, half a dozen stray dogs on the church steps stretched in their sleep, lifted their heads, and rose to trot after the older man.

The *cura* approached the bench, and Kate was introduced. "But we met on your last visit," said the priest. "Is your husband with you?" When there was no answer, he went on, "I shall expect all four of you, then, tomorrow evening at the nuns' school." And when there was still no reply, he said, "At eight o'clock," and the two priests walked away, their habits brushing the cobbles and six gaunt hounds strung out behind.

Kate watched them disappear behind the post office. "In Ibarra even the dogs believe," she said. Then, "Do we have to go? Tomorrow night?"

"We will explain that Steve was detained," said Sara. And when Kate sat on as though the bench had become her newest refuge, Sara started across the street. "Let's go inside the church. It's been repainted."

They mounted the steps, entered the empty nave, and were wholly immersed in blue, the blue of lakes, of water hyacinths, of October noons. Sara and Kate stood on the buckling tile floor as they might at the bottom of the sea.

Encased in glass at the altar stood the Virgin, a plaster statue wearing a filigree crown and a white satin dress.

"Lourdes helps make her clothes," said Sara. "All this is new since last year: the gown, the beaded slippers, the nylon stockings, the rhinestone necklace." She regarded the serene face.

"This Virgin hasn't always been here," Sara said. "She came from a closed chapel in another village and probably, before that, from another one, somewhere else." The figure's calm brown eyes rested on her. Sara added, "All the way back to Spain."

"Then, for her, Ibarra is only a way station," said Kate.

Sara turned to look at her friend. She is becoming perceptive again, Sara thought. I must tell Richard tonight.

They walked into the east transept to look at the statue of the Virgin of Sorrows and into the west transept to look at the painted stations of the cross, then left the church. Standing outside, sunstruck for a moment, they made out the indistinct forms of the *cura,* his assistant, and six dogs coming toward them through the colonnaded shadow of the arcade. And noticed, too, Inocencia on the top step, bundled into all the garments she had ever owned, her hand outstretched.

Sara was reaching into her pocket for a coin when the *cura* came up behind them. "I have remembered something," he said to Kate. "On your husband's last visit he took a colored picture inside the church and promised me a copy. But I never received it." He noticed that Doña Sara's friend, this woman so fair of skin and red of hair, was like a child, easily distracted, a moment ago by the dogs and now by a hornet that, after hanging uncertain at the door, had in a single angry rush entered the nave.

The *cura* went on: "If your husband has the photograph with him, it would be an addition to tomorrow's observance."

Neither woman spoke. The *cura* continued as he might if he had been talking to himself. "Of course, it may have been lost in the mail. Especially if posted as an ordinary letter. To certify is best. Otherwise we risk a loss."

Now he is doing it, and with such authority, thought Sara. That "we" again.

The day of the priests dawned and remained overcast. At noon Sara looked up and said, "It's not usually this cloudy in March."

That evening when they started for the nuns' school, Kate came to the car with her umbrella.

"You won't need that," said Richard. "The first rain of the season isn't due until the twenty-fourth of June, the day of John the Baptist."

"Is it always on schedule?"

"About as often as the train from Juárez. But that's no reason to change the timetable."

Lourdes rode to the village with them, carrying a package wrapped in purple paper. Inside it, she told the Americans, was a tablecloth she had embroidered for the *cura*.

"Does everyone in Ibarra bring a present?" asked Sara.

"Only those who are Catholics."

"You mean everyone except us."

"Except you and two socialists and a communist."

At the nuns' school, two children led the Evertons and Kate the length of the patio, between benches already filled with townspeople. Ahead of them they saw an empty platform and in front of it seven wooden chairs.

From one of these the *cura* rose to introduce the Evertons' guest to his assistant, Padre Javier, and to his aunt, Paulita. Only now, with the Americans assembled, did he notice Steve's absence. Sara opened her mouth to explain, and Richard also seemed about to speak. But Kate broke in before excuses could be made.

"We are parted," she said in her elementary Spanish. *"Estamos partidos."*

Even if the *cura* had correctly heard her say *"partidos,"* he might have misunderstood, for the word could imply separations of any width from a hair's breadth to the vast reaches between the poles. As it was, in the excitement of the moment, he failed to grasp Kate's meaning. Confused by his own exhilaration and her accent, the priest believed her to have said, *"Estamos perdidos,"* and assumed the North Americans were actually lost. As if they were unable to see the seven chairs, he seated the Evertons and Kate one by one, and in the vacant place, without further questions, deposited his own brown overcoat.

Padre Javier, the empty chair, and Richard were on the *cura*'s left; the three women, with Kate in the farthest seat, on his right. The *cura*'s intention had been to divide the men and women into congenial separation, with the two strangers who had difficulty with the language at some distance from himself. Now an unoccupied chair intervened on the men's side, but in any case, the *cura* had things to say privately to Don Ricardo, matters involving repairs at the school, restorations at the monastery, preservation of the church's mosaic dome—all excellent suggestions for the use of mine profits.

The program began with an outpouring of tributes. All those in Ibarra with close connections to religion—the president of *Acción Católica,* the chairman of Catholic Youth, the organist, the sexton, the mother superior of nuns—all stood to certify that without the *cura,* there might be neither church nor chapel in Ibarra, nor a single Catholic to enter them.

Tributes were still being offered when a sudden gust blew in from the street, a hush descended, and rain began to fall. The Evertons looked up into the drizzle as if into the face of a betrayer, and the *cura* reached across Richard for his overcoat. At his right, Paulita, sitting between Sara and Kate, put up her umbrella.

Now, under this precipitation, two dim lamps, and the guidance of a nun, children of the parish school presented two plays. The first one involved a ten-year-old father, a nine-year-old mother, and a doll. But in this drama there followed so many arguments and tears, so many clutchings up and tossings down of the doll, that the plot remained obscure. As a finale, the father tugged a goat onto the platform, the mother said, "Praise God," and the two parents embraced the doll and bowed.

"He has given up cardplaying to become a farmer," Paulita explained to Sara and Kate, who had buttoned their sweaters to the neck and tucked their hands into the sleeves.

Sara turned her head, to see Richard, strands of black hair

limp on his forehead, engaged in conversation with the *cura*. She noticed his unsmiling mouth and how the old scar on his cheek shone white. The priest is asking for something, Sara told herself, but it is no use. Richard will die of pneumonia before the mine can afford the contribution. Beyond her husband and the empty chair, Padre Javier sat with his white head bowed, sleeping as soundly as he would under a roof, on a mattress with two blankets.

Paulita laid her hand, light and brittle as a fallen leaf, on Sara's arm. "It is only sprinkling," she said, "but come closer," and shifting her umbrella, she tried to pull the two North American women under it.

The second play concerned the awakening of faith in a small, shy boy, recognized at once by Sara.

"He's one of Lourdes' grandchildren," she told Kate, who had spread a white handkerchief on top of her head as though it were a shawl, and waterproof.

They watched this child, on his steep ascent to priesthood, mature and age before their eyes, by means of a brief disappearance behind a stone column, where he changed, item by item, from sandals to black shoes, denims to black pants, and added a jacket, hat, and eventually a stiff white collar. Through these various incarnations he was urged on, first by his family, then by his teachers, and finally, when he put on the collar, by his congregation, played by all the other children in the school, who now crowded onto the platform, each carrying a present.

Everyone applauded, the children bowed and disappeared, leaving a pile of vividly wrapped packages behind.

The *cura,* recognizing his cue, rose from his seat and moved forward.

Kate chose this moment to lean in front of Paulita and question Sara. "Where am I to go?" she said, as though she had not noticed the child priest attain his goal step by step but, instead, had sat here, damp and oblivious, planning an itinerary of her own.

"Stay with us longer," Sara said, and, as the *cura* opened his mouth to speak, saw under the limp white handkerchief a negative shake of Kate's head.

The *cura* was explaining the hierarchy of the Church. "There is a direct line," he told the audience. "It leads from you through your priests to the bishop, and from him to the cardinal, and then to the pope, and from the pope to God."

Sara imagined this line extending straight up, like a Hindu rope trick, into the sky over Ibarra, where it intersected the courses of the planets and the patterns of constellations.

"The priests of Ibarra are your spiritual parents," the *cura* said. "The señor Everton and his señora are your material parents."

Sara believed she saw Richard turn pale, and she stood up to leave. With Kate between them, the Evertons left the nuns' school through crowds of expectant faces, already happier and more composed, already better fed.

Kate, rising early the next morning, brought her train ticket to the breakfast table.

"It's for tomorrow," said Richard in a voice grown husky overnight. "From Concepción to Juárez. We should be at the station by six in the evening." He looked up from his plate. "But you're leaving too soon. There are things you haven't seen."

"Yes, stay on," said Sara. But in the end Kate refused their invitations to visit outlying points of interest—the hot springs, the bull ranch, the cathedral in an adjoining state.

"None of them is far from here," said Richard, and, on his way out, left some maps beside Kate's plate. She was still there, alone, looking at maps, when Lourdes arrived for the day.

"How did you like the program?" she asked Kate.

"Very much," said the visitor, and added, "Your grandson is a fine actor."

Lourdes said, "Yes, and he already helps his father mold and fire clay pots."

"How many children do you have?" asked Kate.

"Six," said Lourdes. "Two dead."

Kate reached for her coffee, which had grown cold. "And how many grandchildren?"

"Fourteen. Three dead."

A moment later Kate heard, as she had all her mornings in this house, Lourdes' clear contralto filling the kitchen and the adjoining rooms with song. She sang love songs and songs about places. *"Ay, ay, ay,"* sang the cook.

Before she left for the village that afternoon, Lourdes approached Kate. "Señora, I saw the tickets. Do you mean to leave us?" When Kate nodded, Lourdes shook her head and said, "So soon."

At noon on Friday, Kate heard Sara say, *"Dígame,"* and saw the visitor was Inocencia, asking again for a ride, this time to the railroad station.

"How did she know we were going?"

"As soon as Lourdes left here yesterday afternoon, all of Ibarra knew," said Sara.

That afternoon they drove off at dusk, seated in the car as they had been a week ago. On this trip neither Richard nor Inocencia had anything to say. Kate and Sara each spoke once.

"Lourdes put this in my bag," Kate said, and held up a twist of red thread.

"It is meant to bring you back," said Sara.

When they arrived at the station, two trains, one facing north and one south, were already there, standing on adjacent tracks and preparing for departure.

"The southbound is six hours late," said Richard, "and the northbound half an hour early."

He hired a porter and said to Kate and Sara, "Wait here."

Inocencia had already established herself beside the northbound train, reciting lists of her infirmities at the open windows of day coaches. Through the glass door of the waiting room Sara could see Richard attempting to validate Kate's ticket to Juárez at a counter besieged by hands, peso bills, and protestations.

When she turned back to the platform, Kate had disappeared. Sara ran up to Inocencia. "Where is the North American señora?" But the old woman misunderstood and began to beg from Sara.

The southbound express, on the farther track, was now in motion, was gliding almost silently past a switch to the main line, and when Richard emerged at last from the waiting room with Kate's ticket, all that could be seen of the southbound train was the red lantern at its rear.

At this time Kate's porter, without suitcases or a client, came to the Evertons with a message. The señora had taken the other train. That one. And he pointed down the tracks in the direction of the Mexican states of Jalisco, Guanajuato, and Michoacán. The porter handed the Americans a note.

Using a pencil and a scrap of newspaper, Kate had written, "I've gone on."

On the way back to Ibarra, Inocencia dozed on the back seat, while Sara sat in front and watched stars come out over the mesa.

"But where will Kate go?" she asked her husband.

"It depends on how much she tipped the conductor. Perhaps all the way to Mexico City."

"But if not, if she couldn't make him understand, what then?"

"Then one of the stops between. Felipe Pescador, for instance." And they remembered an old town near a lake gone dry, a town of a church, a bar, and a straggle of farms.

"Or La Chona," said Sara. "It has an inn. And that plaza."

On the moonless road to Ibarra she reminded Richard of the trees in the plaza of La Chona. So ambitious was the gardener that he had clipped a pair of laurels into the crowned figures of Ferdinand and Isabella and then trimmed a tree that faced them into Christopher Columbus presenting his report. And behind Columbus, as though he had brought them along, three leafy ships, the *Niña*, the *Pinta*, and the *Santa María*, sailed up the graveled path.

5

The Watchman at the Gate

It was evident from the start that the two North Americans totally lacked suspicion and were therefore destined to live out their lives handicapped, like accident victims who have lost a leg or infants born deaf. In the village of Ibarra, everyone from the *cura* to the goatherd was of a single opinion, that the señor Everton and his señora had reached maturity oblivious to the envy and greed that, except in rare instances, underlay the nature of man.

The Evertons had been in Ibarra only a month when Luis,

their gardener, proposed that they hire his friend Fermín Díaz as night watchman.

"We do not need a watchman," said Richard. "There is nothing to take."

"There are the cans of food, the bags of fertilizer, and your shoes," Luis said. "And it is widely known that you have lost the key to your front door."

"Perhaps later, when the house is furnished," said the North Americans.

Then Luis spoke again. "You may have forgotten, señor, that Fermín went to work at the age of fifteen in the Malagueña mine for your father's family."

The next day the Evertons engaged Fermín to be the watchman.

On his first night at the gate, Fermín told them, "Those were the happy times, when I worked as an apprentice underground for five pesos a week and was given a sack of corn and a sack of flour to take home on Saturday night. I lived better then than I will today on the salary you have promised, which is twice what my job is worth."

Fermín said he remembered the revolution of 1910 and, groping along the high front wall, found the bullet hole left by Colonel Torres and his men on their way to rob the safe at La Malagueña.

"But this *Coronel* Torres, so proud of his boots and his gun and his stolen horse, had no luck with the safe. The colonel shot at the lock and tried dynamite without success. That night he could not pay his men, and half of them deserted. They crossed the mountains and were on the floor of the valley by morning. But hungry people had been there before them, and the soldiers had to forage for field mice and lizards, and one by one they starved."

"What happened to Torres?" asked Richard.

"*Coronel* Torres fled north to Zacatecas," said Fermín. "He may even have reached Chihuahua, where Pancho Villa was issuing thin wooden slats to use for money. Fifty pesos, *moneda nacional,* he would print on one; one hundred or a thousand pesos on another. Though all the slats a man could carry would not buy a loaf of bread."

The Evertons discovered a low stool, suitable for milking a cow, among the flowerpots on the porch.

Luis explained. "After you are asleep and the house is dark, Fermín sits here until daybreak, in order to protect you against intruders."

"Why not use a comfortable chair?" Richard asked Fermín that evening.

"Because on such a chair I might not stay awake until sunrise," the watchman said. "If I become drowsy on this stool, I immediately fall off and am wide awake again."

"We think you should sleep at least part of the night," first Richard, then Sara told him.

"Then the skunks would tunnel for worms under the honeysuckle, and the coyotes would carry off the hens. Possums and raccoons would gather here. These *mapaches* and *tlacuaches* would inhabit your patio. Wildcats from the mountains could be at home here. Thieves might come."

"There are no thieves," said the Evertons.

Then Fermín filled apertures in the adobe walls with thorny branches of mesquite trees. The North Americans had forbidden him to set traps for either skunks or possums or raccoons, since he had caught a scavenger dog in one and the animal's howls of pain rent the night from one compass point to another.

Luis the gardener, who could tell time within five minutes of the hour by looking at the sun, and Fermín the watchman, who associated many of life's betrayals and rewards with the shifting course of the stars, had been friends since childhood. Luis, being five years younger, had no recollection of Colonel Torres. Instead, he remembered the disappearance of the original bandstand from the plaza of Ibarra.

"The mayor of those days had the *kiosco* carefully dismantled, with all the pieces numbered, and personally sold the carved wood and wrought iron to the magistrate of the town of Tres Glorias," said Luis. "That is how he became rich enough to pursue his career in politics. When I was a child, there were concerts in the plaza every January on the saint's day of this town. All afternoon musicians in red coats played waltzes and polkas behind a grille of iron leaves and iron roses."

"Even without the colonial bandstand and without water to

irrigate the trees, the plaza still has charm," the Evertons insisted.

"It has not," said Luis.

"Where is Tres Glorias?" Richard asked. "Perhaps we will drive over there to see the *kiosco*."

"Tres Glorias is in another state of Mexico," said Luis, in a way that implied the other state was in another hemisphere. Plans for an excursion dwindled and died.

Richard and Sara discovered that Luis was a widower of long standing and Fermín a lifelong bachelor.

"Two lonely old men," Sara said to Lourdes, the cook.

"Luis is not lonely, señora," Lourdes told her. "Though he and the potter are compadres, godfathers of the same child, Luis has been observed since last summer climbing through a window into the room where the potter's wife sleeps."

"Where is the potter?" Sara asked.

Lourdes continued to chop onions in the palm of her hand. "In the cantina," she said, "and after that, asleep on the street halfway home."

Sara recalled returning to the house with Richard after a weekend away and coming upon a man's body spread-eagled on the driveway. At first the two North Americans had failed to recognize the potter and thought that a victim of foul play had been abandoned within their walls.

"You mean the potter is still alive?"

"Yes," said Lourdes, "but he is in poor health."

"Does he know that Luis is with his wife?"

"The potter can no longer separate what he knows from what he dreams," said Lourdes.

Fermín, the watchman, spoke so often of his chest pains and stomachaches and the diminishing number of his days that the Evertons sent him to the doctor in the capital of the state. Fermín returned with a prescription.

"So now you are taking this medicine?" Sara Everton said.

"No, I cannot afford it." Fermín shook his head and his wide-brimmed sombrero.

"We will be happy to pay for it."

"No, señores, I cannot accept further gifts from you."

The Evertons had knowledge of others in the village who earned no more than Fermín and were raising five children, building a lean-to for their stove, and feeding a horse and an orphan lamb.

"But since you have no family, are your expenses actually so great?" Richard asked.

"Señor, it is true," Fermín told him, "that I have never had to pay the cost of a wife."

A silence fell. The night was cold, and Fermín had wrapped himself to the eyes in two deep-fringed *sarapes*. Under the pervading light of the full moon, Sara could see the thongs of his sandals and the broken toenails that protruded from them. Fermín's face was entirely shadowed by the brim of his hat, wide as an oxcart wheel. A truck passed on the road and then a motorcycle.

"However, I do have a child," Fermín said, "at least one child and perhaps two more. That is what she says."

"Who is she?" Sara asked.

"The mother," Fermín told her. "María del Rosario, the mother of my child and the other two that may be mine. Also the mother of seven others, including Ramón, who came here last month to weed. But Ramón is not mine.

"María has ten children, each of a different father, unless it is correct, as the woman insists, that three of them are mine."

Fermín gazed down the road in the direction of Ibarra and went on. "I acknowledge the one child and have consented to pay for her needs." He sighed, and his long nose seemed to grow longer.

"Pay for no more than one," said Richard.

"Does the little girl look like you?" Sara inquired. "Has she your nose and chin?"

At this, Fermín looked up and exposed his gentle, raw-boned face to the moonlight. "My nose, señora? My chin?" And together they started to laugh.

Because Ramón, who came to weed, was fourteen and had never been to school, Sara arranged a meeting with his mother. María del Rosario was a short, cheerful woman, apparently happy with her lot. Although seven of the ten children were old enough for school, none of Sara's arguments in favor of enrollment prevailed. María regarded education as a passing fad of the current administration. In any case, she said, one or two of the older ones must stay with the babies while she was at her work, washing dishes at the café on the plaza.

"As for the others," María said, "who can tell how and where they spend their time? I sometimes notice them at noon, begging from the grocer and the baker."

"Some of the fathers must be helping you," Sara said.

María shook her head. "Not one." Then, seeing the señora's look, she changed this to "Only one."

María said that she and her family lived, not in an ordinary dwelling, but in a narrow thatch-covered space between two houses. She and the ten children shared one room, behind a front wall of rocks and cardboard.

"There are ways to prevent pregnancy without interfering with your normal activities," Sara said. "Have you consulted the doctor at the clinic?" But such a procedure had never occurred to María.

"Surely, when life is so hard, you will not want to bear more children," the North American woman said.

"That is something only the Virgin knows," said María.

Sara looked at her guest. Who am I to attempt to impose common sense on this person? she asked herself. Perhaps I should be like her. She accepts life whole, all of it, as it comes.

With Luis and Fermín in attendance, the Evertons left Ibarra for occasional vacations with confidence, certain that the house and garden would be secure twenty-four hours a day.

But on their return one spring evening from a month's absence, they discovered that Luis was in prison. He had written to Lourdes with messages for them.

"Pues," he wrote. "Well, *mí amíga* Lulu. After you have read this letter, please explain the true circumstances of my arrest to the señor and señora. As you know, from time to time I have grown a few marijuana plants between the nopal cactus behind my house. Only rarely did I profit from this marijuana, which I sold now and then in the form of cigarettes costing five pesos each. Twice I had been warned about this negotiation by agents of the federal government who entered my neighbor's corral and looked over the wall. Each time they confiscated the plants. But I decided to try one more time and soon had my finest crop. I was rolling a few cigarettes one evening when the *federales* came back and burst into my house without permission. 'Luis Fuentes Castillo,' they said, 'you are under arrest.' They drove me directly to the state capital, and the judge sentenced me to be locked up for five years. Please tell all this to the *patrón* and the *patrona* so they will understand why I was not at the gate when they returned. I send to them and to you salutations from my new home, the penitentiary."

So Richard called for the second time on the state prosecutor, as he had in the case of Basilio García, who shot his brother in the back, and again made clear to the attorney the true character and natural innocence of the criminal the government had apprehended. And for the second time the prosecutor agreed to reduce the sentence from five to two years, followed by three on probation.

"Luis is a good man," Fermín said one night, "but he does not recognize those laws he believes to be unjust or impossible to enforce."

A light shone above the door of a small concrete-block structure recently built near the gate.

"How do you like your new house?" Richard asked. "And the cot inside? And the asbestos roof to cover you from thunderstorms?"

"I enter that house only to sweep it," said Fermín. "As for the cot, my grandfather was a Yaqui Indian, and with his blood in my veins I cannot sleep comfortably on anything higher than the ground."

After a pause, Sara spoke. "There are a million stars tonight," she said.

"The heavens are paved with them, señora," said Fermín.

The North Americans hired a youth of sixteen to take the place of Luis in the garden and were amazed at the sudden flowering of roses, the new lushness of ferns, and the increased dimensions of the woodpile.

When Luis was released from the penitentiary, Richard found

him an outside job at the mine, sweeping around the offices and outbuildings.

Prison had returned Luis to Ibarra a thinner man, with fewer teeth and as much gray in his hair as black. But it was apparent from his eyes that abuse and privation had in no way altered his high opinion of life.

Luis's new work allowed him to converse with the miners as they signed in and signed out. He often rested his broom in a doorway and stared across the arroyo, pondering the news they had given him.

One day he initiated a thorough cleanup of the weedy lot behind the storeroom. He first cleared away the brush, then made two piles of what was left. In one he placed objects that would be useful to him—Coca-Cola bottles with refunds due, cardboard boxes and wooden crates in fair condition, a bent saw, and a dozen straight nails. He collected into another heap all the rest—torn paper, splintered boards, oily rags. When the rubbish was gathered together, Luis tossed in a lighted match. A dynamite cap exploded. The detonation knocked him back and dropped him, clothes half torn off, six meters away.

Fermín visited his friend in the hospital.

"From now on Luis will be deaf on one side," Fermín said. "And he can never open his right hand, or close it either. But he will walk and see. He has been granted two separate miracles."

Later on, when Sara Everton returned to Ibarra alone after her husband's death, she visited Fermín at the gate every evening. First they discussed his health, then the weather, the Mexican economy, and the stars.

"There it is," she said, pointing to the east, "the constellation we call Orion in English."

"The four kings and the three Marys," said Fermín.

One night he said, "When you were gone, I had to chase away two boys who were stealing the carved ram's head from the porch. I needed only to say, 'Thieves, you are here at your peril,' and they dropped what they carried and fled, not showing their faces."

"Oh, dear," Sara said.

"So I must ask you to buy me a gun," said Fermín. "A *treinta y ocho especial* like the one I sold the mayor of Ibarra when the señor, your husband, would not allow me to patrol these premises armed. Now you are alone in the house and I am alone outside. With this thirty-eight special I could frighten any *malas personas* who intrude."

"It is hard to tell the bad persons from the friends," Sara objected. "And you have your *machete*. According to Luis, you are faster with it than all the young men of Ibarra."

"Fast to pull it, yes," said Fermín. "But any man in town who is not a cripple can outrun me."

Sara inquired about Luis, who was working a part-time job as watchman at the San Gerónimo mine. Near it he had constructed a low hut, or kennel, out of gunnysacks and newspapers. Into this he crawled when there was frost or hail.

The next morning Sara invited Luis to be at the gate on Sundays, holidays, and Fermín's nights off. Luis not only accepted but was willing to sleep on the watchman's cot.

When she took leave of Fermín at the end of her stay, he said, "Señora, consider this. The front wall is of stone and very high, but the adobe walls at each side of the garden are worn away almost to the ground in places. A child, a goat, or even a pig might enter here, to say nothing of that low element of grown men you regard as friends. In view of this, I must ask you again to buy me a gun."

"No one will harm this house," she said, without explaining that in medieval times, though warlords and traitors and the king of hell himself besieged a citadel, it still held fast when a man known to be beyond reproach stood sentry at the gate.

6

Saint's Day

The sun is scarcely up and coral still streaks the sky over El Nopal when three top-heavy carnival trucks lurch into the village square. They come to a stop outside the *cantina,* which is not yet open for business. Directly across the plaza, the sexton is standing on the church steps with a broom.

Now here come a boy and girl, running, but not to early mass. They want to watch the roustabouts unload the carnival. Before the day is over, they will ride the carousel, or so they believe.

These barefoot children are Paco Ortiz and Gloria Valdés, cousins and lifelong friends. Paco is eight and looks too thin and too old for his age. There is an anxious line between his eyes. Gloria is taller, three years older, and has a dancer's grace and a dancer's flower stem neck, as well as the beginning of full lips and breasts. She is Paco's mother, sister, and unrecognized bride.

Paco's dog, a mongrel bitch, runs after him. Though she is fully grown, she appears to be half-size, her coat matted on her low frame and tangled in a fringe over her glistening eyes. When she was small, Paco named her La Loba, after the female wolf he believed she would eventually resemble.

In the village, the children and the animal are referred to as "the three." "The three are in the arroyo," people say, or "The three are at the well."

Now they wait for the carnival men to set up the rides. The children sit quietly on a bench, while La Loba tracks the gutter right and left in her perpetual search for food. She makes sudden forays on short, shaggy legs to a blackened banana skin or to a scattered heap of corn husks.

More than an hour has passed, and the carousel horses are still roped in the vans, when a long shadow falls across the children from behind. It is Máximo Ortiz, who lays his good hand on his niece's shoulder and his maimed hand on the shoulder of his son. Both turn their heads to look up at him. They see that he is sober. Máximo is known to be the strongest man in El Nopal. Unless he is drunk, he can outreach, outhit, and outrun any man in the village. But since his bad luck, he is not always sober. No sooner did his wife die, bearing the scars he had in-

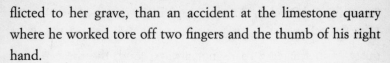

flicted to her grave, than an accident at the limestone quarry where he worked tore off two fingers and the thumb of his right hand.

Now, to remove this hand from his shoulder, Paco stands. "There are the horses. Come on," he says to Gloria, and he practices a whistle he has just learned to summon La Loba.

Máximo watches them approach the trucks, watches La Loba following them, and thinks: I should have killed her two years ago with the rest of the litter. And remembering the annoyances that have plagued his life, along with the great injustices, he allows rage to possess him, lets it burn hot and blind and pure, until at last he strikes the back of the bench and bloodies his good hand.

Paco and Gloria, at the front of a small crowd that is gathering, see that two men have emerged from each cab, pulling away torn sheets of canvas and revealing to the spectators their toppling cargo. They bring four swan boats that will rise and dip not far above the ground, a Ferris wheel, and a carousel. The disassembled frame and the cars of the Ferris wheel fill one truck. In another, the imperial necks of swans are being separated from machinery. The third is apparently entirely filled with the prancing legs of horses. Somewhere among them a golden hoof flashes.

By ten o'clock the crowd has filled the street, but the carnival men are in no hurry. Not a ticket can be sold until after a special twelve o'clock mass to honor the Virgin of Help, the patron saint of this town. To celebrate this mass, the bishop himself is coming from the cathedral in the state capital, seventy-five miles away. And by the time he arrives in his black Buick, which will be dusty from traveling roads not always good, the three palsied motors that operate the rides will already have been set up in the street across from the café and poolroom. Spliced cables will extend out of sight to power lines.

Máximo is not among the spectators. He is on a bench in the middle of the plaza, nursing his throbbing hand. He sees Gloria leave the crowd and start across the square in the direction of her house, where she has left her mother to do all the work alone. She starts to run.

"Stop," says her uncle. "Sit."

She hesitates. He takes her arm and pulls her down beside him. He does not release her hand, which is the color of copper, but holds it on his lap.

"How old are you now?" he says, and she says, "Eleven."

People are passing on their way to find good seats in church. They nod good morning.

"I have to go," says Gloria, and Máximo presses her hand before slowly releasing it.

During the next half hour he first watches the arrival of the bishop, then investigates to see if, by chance, the cantina has opened early. He sees Paco standing so close to the carnival trucks that a roustabout has to tell him to stand back. La Loba is at the boy's feet.

Máximo is back on a bench at twelve o'clock when his sister, Catalina, with Gloria combed and sandaled behind her, hurries past him. For an hour music and prayer and the bishop's voice raised in sermon overflow from the nave of the church into the square, empty now except for Máximo and a few beggars. But by the time mass is over and Catalina and Gloria emerge from the church, Paco is sitting at his father's side, and Máximo holds a large Pepsi in each hand.

He lifts the bottles. "Refreshments for the children," he says.

Catalina, a widow who takes in boarders, examines her brother and sees he has a bloodshot eye, a three-day beard, and a bruise on his lip. She notices his freshly scraped hand and says to herself, Another fight.

Aloud she says, "For a man who lost his wife and his job in one year, you are generous," adding, "and the corn, ripe for the harvest, rotted in last summer's rain."

Máximo holds up his two-fingered hand. "Until a month ago, I was paid for disability."

As she turns away, Catalina says, "You have recovered enough to take light jobs, but instead you loiter all day in the square, a place for children to amuse themselves."

When she is out of sight, Gloria and Paco sit, one on each side of Máximo, and drink their Pepsis without a word. Máximo's left hand lies on the back of the bench behind his son, and his two-fingered right hand rests on his niece's slender thigh.

Gloria is one of God's loveliest creations and still incomplete. Her skin is still a child's, her bones have still to grow. Máximo's hand has discovered that.

When the bottles are empty, Paco is sent to return them to the grocer. But three minutes later he is back. "Come on," he says to Gloria. "They have unloaded the horses. I think there is one that is gold."

Máximo has not removed his hand from Gloria's leg. He is staring at the two dark braids that have fallen forward on her pink sweater. He sees that his niece has been growing so fast that three pearl buttons have been pulled off. Gloria is looking up at him.

"Go ahead," he says. "Choose the horse you will ride to-night." He watches her move with head high through the crowd. She is barefoot again.

It is already two in the afternoon, and the horses still lie on their sides on the floor of the carousel. Even in this position they are rearing, plunging, and opening their blood-red mouths to bare the bit between their fierce ivory teeth.

"Here it is," says Paco.

He is looking at a charger as black as night, its mane whipped back by a savage gale, its bulging eyes fixed on glory. Its reins and saddle are gem-studded, and its four golden hoofs strike hard at the air. Now the men who are setting the horses in place pierce each one with a golden pole.

Gloria and Paco turn as Máximo comes up behind them. "Later on, I will buy you each a ride," he says.

Gloria is leaning back against a folded ladder. Her half-unbuttoned sweater gapes between young breasts that are still no more than promises.

"Your mother wants you," the uncle tells his niece at last. "There are clothes to wash." Then he calls her back as she starts away. "But meet me here at five o'clock. For your ride."

At the same time, Paco leaves the plaza to engage in business. He will spend the afternoon searching El Nopal for empty bottles and, later on, collect from the grocer the refunds due. In this way he can pay for a ticket or two on the carnival rides. Even if his father remembers the ticket he promised, Paco already knows that one will not be enough.

So until dusk, Paco, dragging a sack and tagged by La Loba, walks the stony streets of the town as if he were a stranger here, with his head down, looking from left to right, moving from dusty lane to dusty lane and circling back again. Three times he rounds the post office and three times the house of the widow Ortega, who sells goat's milk. He hunts bottles as far as the thatched lean-to of old Josefina, who performs cures, and as far as the baseball field. La Loba is at his heels.

Paco is about to return to the plaza with eighteen bottles for refunds, when La Loba suddenly yelps in pain. But it is more than a yelp. It is a sustained howl, carried on a single high note that paralyzes time and makes the air too cold to breathe. Paco turns to see his father looming tall behind him. Máximo holds a second stone in his good hand. La Loba, dragging one of her hind legs, has crawled to the protection of the thorned mesquite bush. Her moans diminish.

"Your dog was after that hen," Máximo says, and points to a stringy pullet, cackling and running in maddened zigzags from one side of the road to the other. "I can't afford to pay the owner for a dead chicken." Now he notices Paco's sack. "But perhaps you can." He counts the bottles.

He fingers the stone in his hand, then tosses it away, allowing it to fall short of La Loba. He feels regret for the second time that day.

"She should have died with the rest of the litter," he says.

Paco remembers the occasion well. This litter, of which La Loba is the sole survivor, perished at Máximo's hand two years before. Paco was six then, and his mother, a frail, fearful woman, was still alive. She lived in grief, orphaned as she was by the deaths of the three children who had followed Paco. On the day of the killing, Paco, as soon as he perceived his father's intentions, had run to his mother for help. She neither looked at him nor moved from where she sat on the edge of the bed, her elbows on her knees, her thin fingers pressed to her eyes, rocking back and forth, as if the rocking itself might serve for something. As if it, more than tears, might speak for her.

So Paco by himself attempted to stay his father's arm as Máximo carried the five young animals into the corner of the corral. Here he took them, one after another, by their hind legs, which had bones no bigger than a quail's, swung them high, and brought their heads down sharp and hard against the wall.

Paco watched the blood splatter and screamed so loud that old Walterio, who lived next door and was eighty-seven, put his head over the wall, regarded the scene, and said, "Wait."

Four of the litter already lay dead in the dirt, and the fifth was shivering and dripping in Máximo's hand, when old Walterio said, "Stop. What is the matter with him?" And he pointed to Paco, who clung with such determination to his father's arm that he was lifted, still weeping, off his feet and into the air.

Receiving no answer, Walterio exercised the authority of his years and said to Máximo, "Give that animal to the child, and let us put an end to the disturbance."

Máximo, reflecting that Walterio was his mother's cousin and that the dog might develop a nose for game and be of some use, shrugged and handed La Loba to Paco.

Then Walterio said, "Peace is God's gift to the aged. Remember that," and disappeared.

Now, on the saint's day of El Nopal, with the church bells about to ring for vespers and La Loba fully grown, Paco decides to stop at old Walterio's house to show him the dog.

Old Walterio has forgotten everything. "Whose animal is that?" he says, and to Paco, "What's your name?"

When Paco explains, "I am the son of Máximo," all old Walterio says is, "Who?"

At this same time Máximo is calling at his sister's house. They talk in the doorway. Over Catalina's shoulder, Máximo can see Gloria, in her open pink sweater, ironing the boarders' shirts.

"Come outside," Máximo tells his sister. Catalina already knows that he is going to ask for money, and that she will give him some, even if he intends to cheat her, even if he lies. Even if, so early in the evening, he smells of *mescal*.

Máximo is stringing together his fictions.

"A friend of mine is here today," he says, and speaks a name. "He is offering me work on a ranch he owns, fifty kilometers to the south." And Catalina regards him silently, watching him invent.

Máximo goes on. "The property is modest in size, the work is light." He pauses, and they both wait to find out what he will say next. "There is a spring of pure water located a shadow's length from the house."

Catalina believes in neither the friend nor the ranch, and least of all in the pure spring water, but the fact that her brother has dared to present this dream to her, the fact that he can fabricate a tale of such good luck, revives memories of him as a child. In those days he boasted of a future when he would fight bulls, race cars, and be paid to dive from cliffs into the sea.

Observing him on this feast day of the Virgin of Help in the town of El Nopal, Catalina recognizes in her brother the thwarted, sullen boy he used to be. For an instant and against her will, she pities him.

Then she brings fifty pesos from her house, hands the money to Máximo, and watches his anger mount. He hurls the bills to the ground.

When Catalina says, "I can give you no more," she expects him to strike her, but he only pockets the bills, turns his back, and walks off without a word. Catalina contemplates him. Perhaps the problem is only a woman. Perhaps all he wants is money to pay a woman for the night.

On his way home, Máximo stops at a carnival booth that displays dolls and toy guns, straw hats and tooled belts, jewelry and perfume. He buys a rhinestone necklace and carries it away in a twist of pink tissue paper.

At five o'clock he meets Paco and Gloria in the plaza. La Loba, exhilarated by the crowds, reconnoiters in all directions, her tail curled tight. The three carnival rides are strung with bulbs of all colors, and waltzes swing and dip from the calliope at the center of the carousel. The Ferris wheel, the swans, and the horses have been revolving since midafternoon, but now, at dusk, before the children's eyes, they take on the aspect of magic.

Máximo buys two tickets for the swans and from the sidelines watches Gloria and Paco soar and sink and soar again. Then they go on to the Ferris wheel, where they have to wait for places.

Paco's hand is in his pocket, guarding the two pesos he collected for the empty bottles. Máximo buys three tickets and, when they are allowed to board, he sits with Gloria, while Paco finds a place next to a fat man in the car behind. When Paco's car has to wait at the top for passengers to get in at the bottom, he sees the whole town of El Nopal, its church, its square, its post office and school. As they descend, he looks into the car ahead, where his father's right arm is around Gloria's shoulder and his left holds both of hers between his knees. Gloria sits still as a statue. Paco understands that she is frightened of the wheel.

When the ride is over, Máximo says, "Once again," to the ticket taker, but he buys only two tickets, so Paco must dig into his pocket for one of the pesos he is saving for the carousel. The ride is the same this time. The fat man rocks the car, the operator shouts, Máximo's arm by now completely encircles Gloria, and the music of the carousel absorbs all other sounds.

Their ride is over and the wheel stops, but Máximo says, "One more time," and again buys two tickets. Paco thinks of the carousel and hesitates, but as the wheel begins to turn, he pays with his last peso for the ride.

Five minutes later Máximo and the children are in the square again, back of the bandstand, away from the crowd. Paco's father tells him, "Wait here. Gloria wants to go home." When Paco and La Loba still trail him, he waves them back.

"Will you buy tickets for the carousel?" Paco asks, and his father turns to say, "Why not? Trust me." The two start off in the direction of Catalina's house. Paco and La Loba immediately rejoin the crowd.

Now the clock in the church tower strikes seven, and Máximo has not returned. The bishop left in his big black car three hours ago, and the carnival will travel on tonight.

After fifteen minutes, Paco goes to the ticket seller in front of the carousel.

"How long will you operate the horses?"

"Until eight o'clock," says the man. "The carnival closes at eight."

Paco runs home, with La Loba panting behind. He opens the door into the first room, which is the *sala,* the kitchen, and his bedroom. It is dark, but there is a slit of light under the door to his father's room. Paco listens at the threshold and hears nothing. He pushes the door ajar and sees by the low flame of an oil lamp that his father and Gloria are there.

Gloria lies quiet on the mattress, with her shoes and sweater off. Máximo is at her side, with the palm and two fingers of his right hand across her mouth. His left hand pulls at the buckle of his belt and the fastener of his denim pants. Máximo and Gloria do not see Paco. His father's back is turned, and Gloria's head is twisted so that she can look only at the ceiling, which is stained by last summer's rains. There is a piece of pink paper on the floor.

Paco has silently closed the bedroom door and is crossing the outer room without a sound when he hears the ring of metal on the tile floor. When there is silence again, he enters that room and again is not seen. Máximo's denim pants are on the floor, also a five-peso coin, escaped from a pocket and gleaming under the lamp. Paco does not look in the direction of the bed, from which the only sound is his father's harsh breathing.

It is only when he reaches the outer door with the coin in his hand that he hears Gloria. He recognizes the sound she is making. La Loba made the same sound a few hours earlier, when Máximo stoned her. Fear, cold as a knife blade, slices into Paco's heart.

But as soon as he starts toward the plaza, he hears only his own running feet and the panting of the dog behind.

The carousel is about to close. Leaving La Loba to prowl as she pleases, Paco buys five tickets at the booth and takes the reins of his coal-black, gold-shod steed. He breathes in cold night air, deafened by the calliope, blinded by the lights. He believes with each successive ride that he is making wider and wider turns. He swings away from the saddle dangerously, leaning into the dark. When he leans far enough, he sees La Loba looking up at him from under a sidewalk bench.

The hands of the clock are almost at eight when the conductor collects Paco's last ticket and signals the operator. The motor starts, the calliope blares, the conductor slaps Paco's black mount on its shiny rear and, when the turntable is already in motion, steps off it backward into the crowd.

Now, for five minutes, Paco is a child without a past. This interval contains his whole life. So his day ends almost as he had planned, riding a horse to music under stars.

Part IV

Memory

1

Please

If you see a pale-pink chiffon evening dress, circa 1928, the low waist caught at one side by full-blown pink silk roses, in the nostalgia department of wherever you shop, please let me know.

If you run across an original recording of Chaliapin singing "The Flea," Galli-Curci singing "Caro Nome," or Marion Harris singing "It Had to Be You," please buy it for me. Also, anything played by Rachmaninoff or Gabrilowitsch.

In one of those catchall used-book stores, while looking for Updike and Salinger in hardback, you may uncover a collection of old theater programs. Please reserve the following for me: any performance of Max Reinhardt's *Miracle*, and the Orpheum bill with either Houdini or Sarah Bernhardt in the main act. General deterioration of pages is not a consideration.

When you're at the beach, hanging on to your board, your fins, your towel, your book, and your beer, as you make your way over a field of human flesh, please see the sand as empty, endless, silent, clean. Please notice eight gulls drilling for crabs in the shallow water. Please look beyond the unmolested surf to your vision's final boundary, where the deepest and brightest blue runs into the lighter sky. There are two boats, a fishing launch in plain view and a freighter on the horizon. You presume it is a freighter. You presume it is the horizon.

Please drive from your house to the foot of the mountains. The only structures in sight are occasional white frame farmhouses set close to long red barns. Now leave your car and climb across the granite boulders of a dry arroyo. You walk toward an oak tree in an unplowed field and flush a quail. You part a knee-high sea of yellow, orange, and blue. Please don't pick the flowers.

2

Low Tide at Four

What I remember of those summers at the beach is that every afternoon there was a low tide at four.

I am wrong, of course. Memory has outstripped reality. But before me as I write, in all its original colors, is a scene I painted and framed and now, almost fifty years later, bring to light.

Here, then, is a California beach in summer, with children, surfers, fishermen, and gulls. The children are seven and three. We are on the sand, a whole family—father, mother, a boy and a girl. The year is 1939. It is noon. There will be a low tide at four.

Days at the beach are all the same. It is hard to tell one from another. We walk down from our house on the side of the hill and stop on the bluff to count the fishermen (five) on the pier and the surfers (three), riding the swells, waiting for their waves. We turn into Mrs. Tustin's pergola restaurant for hamburgers. Though we recognize them as the best in the world, we never eat them under the matted honeysuckle of the pergola. Instead, we carry them, along with towels, buckets, shovels, books, and an umbrella, down the perilous, tilting wooden stairs to the beach. Later we go back to the pergola for chocolate and vanilla cones.

"Ice cream special, cherry mint ripple," says Mrs. Tustin on this particular day, and we watch a fat man lick a scoop of it from his cone. We wait for him to say, "Not bad," or "I'll try anything once," but he has no comment. A long freight train rattles by on the tracks behind the pergola.

As we turn away, Mrs. Tustin says, "The world's in big trouble," and the fat man says, "You can say that again. How about that paperhanger, Adolf?" But it is hard to hear because of the train.

Back on the beach, our heads under the umbrella, we lie at compass points like a four-pointed star. The sun hangs hot and high. Small gusts of wind lift the children's corn-straw hair. We taste salt. Face down, arms wide, we cling to the revolving earth.

Now Mr. Bray, the station agent, a middle-aged Mercury in

a shiny suit, crosses the dry sand in his brown oxford shoes. He is delivering a telegram. Everyone listens while I read the message from our best and oldest friends. Sorry, they can't come next weekend after all. Good, we say to ourselves, without shame.

I invite Mr. Bray to join us under the umbrella. "Can't you stay on the beach for a while?" He pauses with sand sifting into his shoes. Oh, no, he has to get back to his trains. He left his wife in charge, and the new diesel streamliner will be coming through.

At this moment a single-seated fighter plane from the navy base north of us bursts into sight along the shore, flying so low it has to climb to miss the pier. The children jump into the air and wave. The pilot, who looks too young for his job, waves back.

"Look at that," says Mr. Bray. "He could get himself killed."

Time and the afternoon are running out. A fisherman reels in a corbina. Three gulls ride the swells under the pier. The children, streaked with wet sand, dig a series of parallel and intersecting trenches into the ebb tide. Their father walks to the end of the pier, dives into a swell, rides in on a wave, and walks out to the end of the pier again. I swim and come back to my towel to read. I swim and read again.

Winesburg, Ohio; Sister Carrie; Absalom, Absalom; Ethan Frome; The Magic Mountain; Studs Lonigan; A Handful of Dust; A Room with a View. There are never books enough or days enough to read them.

I look up from my page. Here is old Mrs. Winfield's car being parked at the top of the bluff. It must be almost four. Her combination driver, gardener, and general manager, Tom Yoshimura, helps her into a canvas chair he has set up in front of the view. His wife, Hatsu, new from Japan, is stringing beans for dinner in Mrs. Winfield's shingled house on the hill. Hatsu can't speak English. She bows good morning and good afternoon.

Mrs. Winfield has survived everything: her husband's death and the death of a child, earthquakes, floods, and fires, surgical operations and dental work, the accidents and occasional arrests of her grandchildren. All these, as well as intervals of a joy so intense it can no longer be remembered. I watch Tom Yoshimura bring her an ice cream cone from the pergola.

It is four o'clock. We are standing in shallow water at low tide. The children dig with their toes and let the waves wash in and out over their feet. They are sinking deeper and deeper. During the summer, their skins have turned every shade of honey: wildflower, orange, buckwheat, clover. Now they are sage. I look into my husband's face. He reaches over their heads to touch my arm.

At this time on this August day in 1939, I call up my interior reserves and gather strength from my blood and bones. Exerting the full force of my will, I command the earth to leave off circling long enough to hold up the sun, hold back the wave. Long enough for me to paint and frame low tide.

3

Like Heaven

Late on a September afternoon, with barely time for a side trip before dark, Elizabeth Troy left the main highway and followed a winding road to a seaside town she used to know. Once there, she found its light and sound, its single wooded hill, its mile of beach, now widening at low tide, so improbably familiar that at first she thought she was lost. The rack of sunglasses in the drugstore window, the flag on the grocery, the pines and eucalyptus on the hill across the road, the whole look of the place, struck her as magic, a triumph of recollection over reality.

Standing on the cement walk that ran for only a block and a

half, breathing air that came quick and blue from the sea, she was glad she was here, a few miles west of the freeway, in a place she hadn't seen for fifteen years.

She parked in front of a vacant lot, in case the Alvarado brothers and Mrs. Nye still owned their stores and might notice and recognize her, then waste time talking. She thought she had glimpsed a dark Alvarado head behind the meat counter of the grocery and Mrs. Nye's glasses gleaming behind the drugstore counter.

Beyond Elizabeth, the pink stucco post office was closing for the night. A border of nasturtiums erupted against its side in hot reds and lemon yellows, the intense shades that figure more often in memory than in fact. Elizabeth turned to face the ocean.

Here there was a change. The end of the pier had broken off and taken with it four fishermen's benches and a bait house. A life preserver still hung from a loose guardrail. Elizabeth watched a jogger run north on the beach and two others pass him, running south.

Footsteps approached and stopped. It was an Alvarado brother, the oldest one, Juan, who had never learned much English.

"Juan," she said, and shook hands.

Juan said, "Welcome," and smiled the wide smile she remembered.

"I'm only passing through," she said.

"Then you live here now," said Juan.

"I have to leave before dark."

"Which is your house?"

"No, I'm just passing through."

"Welcome," said Juan, and they shook hands again.

Now there was less than an hour of daylight left. Elizabeth crossed the street, passed the closed Unitarian church and the closed real estate office, and walked down Seaside to Pine. Pine Street climbed the hill in the rough shape of a question mark and shone with a recent coat of tar. Unpaved lanes ran off it.

At the second crossroad, Elizabeth turned right. This had been a street of garage studios and houses split into apartments. Couples halfway between her age and her mother's used to rent here by the month in the summer. During the week, the wives took care of one or two small children, rinsing sand from their hair, pulling up blankets at night. The husbands came for weekends, and on Friday night and Saturday, couples went from house to house, carrying corn chips and glasses out of which martinis splashed to dot the dust of the lane. Sometimes, over the weekend, the composition of the couples changed and new pairs formed, only to regroup by six o'clock Sunday into the original pairs—the father and mother of the child who, bathed, combed, and bearded with cookie crumbs, was already learning to survive.

Sometimes the halves of couples failed to rejoin. This happened in the case of Elizabeth's cousin Jane, who left her new husband for someone's houseguest so suddenly that her eggplant casserole was still in the oven and her wet two-piece bathing suit still on the line.

Today, towels hung from the balcony of one apartment. A motorcycle stood at the front door of another. Four had signs offering them for winter rent, and a converted garage was for sale.

Elizabeth, continuing up Pine, paused on the curve to look back at the cobalt sea, then turned in the direction of the house where she had spent her summers as a girl. Scuffing through pine needles, she passed a row of compact new houses before she came to one she recognized. It had belonged to Captain Benton-Smith, who was wounded in the first attack on Gallipoli in 1915 and spent twenty-four hours bleeding on the beach. The captain's scars were visible when, before taking his swim, he sat on the sand in his panama hat and the black trunks that came to his knees. His cheerful nature and reasonable attitude toward the rout ("We should have given the buggers a shot at the generals") turned the white cavities carved out of his neck and shoulders into metaphors of scars, acquired without pain or fear.

The captain spent all his summers here, attended to by Irish Meg, a woman of such a frank green gaze and broad white smile that everyone assumed he loved her and, hale as he was, took her regularly to bed. Now ice plant overran Captain Benton-

Smith's lawn, and ivy wound its way through the louvered shutters of his house.

Beyond two more new cottages, Elizabeth came to the Scotts' and the Mannings' houses. Mrs. Scott and Mrs. Manning had been amateur botanists. They spent their summers hatted and scarved, on top of the hill or on the slopes behind it, carrying sketch pads and crayons and, in a hamper, watercress-and-cucumber sandwiches and a flask of sherry. At the end of the summer, one year in one house, the next in the other, they exhibited their drawings, spidery and faint, of blossoms, nettles, and varieties of sage.

The Potters' house stood on a rise above a canyon that was dense with underbrush and the shade of trees. Annie Potter and Elizabeth had been best summer friends in the years before college. Then one went east and one went north and they began to like other people. Annie became a painter and eventually married one. Now she lived in Napa Valley.

There had been a time when Elizabeth and Annie Potter, day after day, had stretched out, wet from the ocean, to lie for hours on adjacent towels on the sand. They had spent a large part of ten summers this way, flat on their stomachs or their backs, in talk, in silence, and in talk again.

Annie's uncle Si, her father's handsome younger brother, had usually spent August here and was the second hero on the street.

Uncle Si went into World War II a year before necessary. At twenty, he flew a Spitfire for the British over the Sussex Downs and Kent. The next year he was with the Americans over North Africa. He was shot down twice and came home with medals and oak leaf clusters. Once, when Elizabeth was sitting with Annie on the Potters' fringed porch swing, Uncle Si happened to say, as if the strip of ocean he could see between two pines had reminded him of it, that he had known one or two American pilots who tried to shoot down their own fighters. He said he was almost picked off by a flier in his squadron who wanted to claim a hit on a German bomber as his own. "To improve his score," said Uncle Si, "and get home sooner." He said this and laughed. Uncle Si's looks set him apart. And when jokes were told, it was Uncle Si who always laughed the longest.

Beyond the Potters' rambling one-story, in front of the house where she herself had spent so many summers, Elizabeth came face-to-face with Mr. Elby. She remembered him, a master of ingenious household repairs, as if they had met yesterday. He was pushing a bicycle that he appeared much too old to ride. His nose was thinner than when she had seen him last, his eyes hollower, and his ears almost transparent.

With his faded stare on her, Elizabeth stopped and said hello.

"You're Lizzie," Mr. Elby said, and she saw that a front tooth, missing fifteen years ago, had never been replaced.

This meeting would delay her. Now she might not get to the top of the hill and down to the beach before dark. "How are you, Mr. Elby?" she said.

"Good," he said. He examined her for changes—a few white hairs, perhaps, a thickening waist. Then he said, "You look all right. You're still wiry." He held his bicycle, ready to mount. "How's that man of yours, what's-his-name?"

"Greg," said Elizabeth, and paused. She had lived too close to her husband for too long to sum him up on such short notice. Without speaking, she continued to stare at Mr. Elby, who had once shot a skunk from her mother's bedroom window. ("I can get a better bead on it from here.")

"Well, Greg, how's he?" Mr. Elby persisted.

When she still stood silent, Mr. Elby made a guess. "He's gone," he said soberly.

"Not really," she said. "But he's away. He's in Mexico."

"One of them places," said Mr. Elby. Then, "I never got to know him like I do you."

"Perhaps you will sometime." She might as well have said, Perhaps a tidal wave will leave fishes gasping on Pine Street. "He has to be at meetings," Elizabeth told Mr. Elby, and could have added, My husband is trying to save the world. She placed Greg in conference, this time in a colonial building that had an interior carved stone balustrade and carved lintels at its windows. Under the windows, starving people lined the curb.

"What kind of meetings are those?"

"Scientific," she said. "Better ways to grow food."

"I lost all my tomatoes to the beetle," said Mr. Elby. "Where've you been, anyway? How are the kids?"

Elizabeth answered the questions in order. "Lately in Mexico," she said. Then, "They're both in college and fine." She silently added, I hope. There was no way of telling how they were, out of sight and growing up too fast.

"You living here?" Mr. Elby asked with suspicion. If she had rented one of these houses without telling him, he would resent the lost chance to check the gas outlets and get the rust out of the pipes.

"I wish I could." Then she spoke to Mr. Elby as she once would have to Annie Potter. "It would be like heaven."

"Like heaven," he repeated, and was silent for a moment. "Maybe so, maybe not." He propped his bicycle against the choked honeysuckle on the fence. A light fragrance rose from the matted flowers. "What did you come for?" he asked.

Elizabeth sensed that she was under interrogation. "Why did you do it?" prosecutors asked criminals, parents asked children. "Why?" Greg had asked. "Why do you count the beggars and not the free breakfasts in the schools? Why mourn all the losses and never celebrate the gains?"

She had tried to answer. "Because people in rags pray in churches decorated with gold leaf, because little boys fight to clean your windshield for five cents, because families gather to sift the garbage heaps," she told him.

Now here was Mr. Elby asking why she had come back. She told the truth. She said, "I don't know." Then added, "Who knows when I can come again? We're in Mexico to stay." She superimposed on the hillside where she stood a different landscape, a waste of depleted earth and shriveled grain. Greg had taken her to such places and later to an experimental patch of fertile ground, where he stripped an ear of corn and exposed the fat, even kernels.

"Look at this," he told her, as if this single ear could multiply until it fed every man, woman, and child on earth.

He watched her face. "You don't believe it will happen," Greg said. "Why?"

Elizabeth only said, "Remember the summers at the beach? Everyone in town had enough to eat. They were all happy," and she thought of ocean sunlight on a hundred happy faces.

But the last time Greg tried to convince her of the approaching utopia, she had answered, "Someday you'll make me believe it," and, standing between the rows of corn, had flung her arms around his neck.

To Mr. Elby she said, "Greg is inventing a new kind of corn."

Mr. Elby had nothing to say about the diet of Mexico. He nodded as if, all along, he had expected her to settle there.

Elizabeth gazed at the gray-shingled house, the summer site of her growing up. It needed repairs. Paint, at least. Perhaps a new roof.

"Is it empty?" she asked.

"There's a lease on it," he said. "One of them teachers from the new state college down the coast." A smile struggled to lift the corners of Mr. Elby's mouth. "And the heater leaking water and the oven leaking gas and the faucets . . ." He was approaching a delirium of satisfaction.

Elizabeth interrupted. "How about the Mannings and the Scotts?"

Mr. Elby collected himself. They faced one another on the road, the level rays of the declining sun still bright on Elizabeth's left side, Mr. Elby's right.

"The Scotts, they're gone. Haven't seen the Mannings or the Millers or the what's-their-names, the ones who had the boy that liked dogs. Seems like he always had a stray tagging after him."

Mr. Elby was speaking of Billy Morton, and Elizabeth already knew what had become of Billy. His parents were among the friends she hadn't lost.

"Do you remember the time you shot the skunk from that window?" She pointed to a corner of the house.

Mr. Elby flushed with anger. "I never shot a skunk," he said.

Silence fell. Elizabeth picked a leaf of rosemary from a bush gone wild at the edge of the lane. She and Mr. Elby moved out of the way of a passing car. The driver waved and turned into the Potters' drive.

"Another teacher," said Mr. Elby. "Wait till the old wiring blows a fuse." His voice grew firm in anticipation.

"I wanted to go up to the cabin," Elizabeth told him, and corrected herself. "Up to where the cabin used to be."

"I guess you heard about the fire." Mr. Elby shook his head. "Some of these kids ought to be run in."

Elizabeth rolled the rosemary leaf between her fingers and smelled it. Immediately, all her relinquished summers were restored, the ones before Greg, the ones with Greg, with one child, with two children. The cabin, built quickly and cheaply, had been a firetrap all along, she supposed. It was simple good luck that the place burned with no one in it. Even so, as she thought now of the sand between the children's sheets, of the hermit crabs surviving overnight in jars, of the shells in a bucket and the sage in a glass, of the intimacy and isolation of the raw wood structure, Elizabeth suffered a pang. All four of them had been so young. For a second, looking backward, she believed she remembered exactly how it had felt.

But Mr. Elby was thinking about the fire. "These kids," he said. "Do yours take drugs?"

"I'm not sure," Elizabeth said truthfully. The sea shone silver blue between the pines. "I have to go now. I have to get down to the beach."

Mr. Elby nodded, as if wanting to be on the beach was always reasonable, in any season, at any hour. "It's low tide about now," he said.

At the moment of parting, she remembered to ask, "How's Mrs. Elby?"

"She's gone." Mr. Elby pulled his bicycle out of the honeysuckle. "It's been seven years. Seven or eight." His eyes began to water. "She's in that new cemetery." He gestured to an unseen location behind the hill. "Seems like I can't keep flowers growing on her grave. The ground squirrels get them."

His voice was shaking. Without saying goodbye, he mounted his bicycle, wavered, righted himself, and, sitting taller than Elizabeth would have thought possible, pedaled out of sight.

Half an hour was left before sunset. To save time she took a shortcut down the hill, through the canyon that was littered with eucalyptus pods and bark. At the intersection of Seaside and Pine, the business block on the west cast shadows halfway across the main street. Elizabeth tried to skirt the drugstore without being seen, but Mrs. Nye, on the lookout, tapped on the plate glass with her pen. Elizabeth turned back.

An apothecary jar, filled with amethyst liquid, stood as it always had in a curtained alcove to the left of the door. The changeless display of dark glasses and sand toys crowded the window to her right.

Inside the store, Mrs. Nye examined her through both the upper and lower lenses of her bifocals. "You're looking pretty good, Lizzie. You're young yet."

Mrs. Nye had trapped her new permanent in a beaded hair net. "Are you back to stay?" she asked.

"How could I? Someone's burned the cabin down."

"No one burned it down," Mrs. Nye said. "There was a brush fire up there."

"I guess Mr. Elby forgot."

"You've been talking to Bert." Then Mrs. Nye, as though the month were June, carried a beach umbrella to the window. "Bert Elby hasn't been the same since his wife died. Sometimes he can't tell the difference between now and the year before last." She passed Elizabeth a carton of chocolate bars and unwrapped one for herself. "They had to take his gun away after he mistook a kid's loose hamster for a rat."

Elizabeth supposed Mr. Elby was eighty. It was harder to tell about Mrs. Nye. She was one of those women, double-chinned and sane, who, once past fifty, never change.

"What did Bert tell you?" she asked Elizabeth.

"About everyone dying or moving away, the Scotts and Mannings and Mortons. I forgot to ask about the Potters. He spoke about college professors who live in the houses."

"The Lord God sent those professors to keep us going," said Mrs. Nye. "They don't pack up and get out on Labor Day."

Elizabeth deciphered the time from a wall clock painted over with a clipper under sail. "It's late," she said, and edged away. "I have to see the beach again, while there's still light."

Mrs. Nye stopped her. "Wait a minute," she said. "I want to tell you what's what."

Leaning over the counter between twin pyramids of sun oil and shampoo, she brought Elizabeth up-to-date.

"Mrs. Scott's here now with her grandson. Mrs. Manning came down in August with her nurse. The captain's been gone a long time. Mr. Si Potter's dead. His car hit a tree on a straight piece of road in broad daylight. He always did drive too fast." Elizabeth had a second to think, He must have meant to die. Mrs. Nye passed the chocolate bars again. "Annie Potter, that friend of yours, comes once in a while with her two kids. When the marriage broke up, they split up four kids. He got two and she got two. She rents the loft over the Millers' garage."

Elizabeth, fleeing further news, had reached the door. She said goodbye. "Thank you for the candy," she said, as she so often had in childhood. Her foot was on the sidewalk. The shadows of the stores had stretched across the road.

But Mrs. Nye had more to say. "You probably heard about the Morton boy. Hit when he was riding his motorcycle on the freeway." She paused to remember Billy. "Whenever he came in here, he left some dog or other barking outside the door for him."

Elizabeth stepped onto the sidewalk. Sunlight was fading from the roofs on the hill.

Mrs. Nye called after her. "I forgot to ask about your kids."

"They're fine," said Elizabeth. But the children were thousands of miles away. She had no proof.

"And that Greg you married?" Mrs. Nye looked sharply at Elizabeth. "Are you two still married?"

Elizabeth nodded. "We live in Mexico," she said, offering the remark as an explanation of anything and everything Mrs. Nye might want to know. She imagined Greg at tomorrow's confer- ence, in a room with tall windows, a French chandelier, and a tilting parquet floor. Behind him pressed the starving millions.

"What does he do?" called Mrs. Nye.

"Hungry people," Elizabeth called back. She waved and walked into a gust of salt air.

Before arriving at the wooden stairs that led down the bluff to the sand, she had time to wonder if anything she had just heard was true. Mrs. Nye had made at least one mistake. Billy Morton didn't die on the reaches of pavement of Interstate 10. Seven months after his high school graduation, he was killed in an ambush in Vietnam. The brief obituary named his parents as survivors. There would be no services, the paper said. Gifts to the Humane Society were suggested.

At the top of the steps, Elizabeth clung to the rusty iron rail. The Humane Society! she silently exclaimed.

The sun, round and huge and orange, was only inches above the horizon. Elizabeth left her shoes on the lowest step and walked barefoot toward the water across a gleaming landscape of wet sand, passing the exposed piles of what remained of the pier. She stood at the ocean's edge while shallow waves rippled in and left circles of foam around her feet. Twisting, she looked back at the hill. Once it had been easy to see the cabin from here. She imagined she saw the chimney now, a blackened square against the sky.

Life on the hill had not been flawless. Elizabeth vaguely recalled the occasional tears of children and slammings of adult doors. But the immense peace of the place drowned out these events, leaving only a shimmering calm behind. Under its protection, summer days could scarcely be told apart and ran together. So that, even while being lived, they had seemed eternal.

From where she stood now, Elizabeth had watched another sunset fifteen years ago. Then she had a child at each side, with the shadows of giants lengthening behind them. Not far away, Greg talked to a lifeguard, who was scanning the surf with binoculars. A boat had capsized that morning, and two fishermen were missing. When seaweed drifted against Elizabeth's foot, she started. She had expected a torn sock or the sole of a shoe.

Aside from that, it had been an evening much like this one, of singular perfection. Like now, the final second of the day hung on a sliver of sun. Sandpipers had tracked the margin of the sea. The lifeguard's binoculars had tracked the breakers.

Now Elizabeth felt a sudden thudding on the sand. A few feet behind her, a solitary jogger ran north. Fifty yards farther up the beach, a boy carrying swim fins walked out of the waves and headed for the steps. She supposed he was Mrs. Scott's grandson, aged about sixteen, lean of build and badly sunburned, his wet hair plastered to his face. Elizabeth saw him smile as he came near. Then his happiness spilled over, and he spoke.

"How about this?" he said. "How about it?" Turning, he lifted his hand to the sky, the shore, the water, her.

4

A Sleeve of Rain

Sometimes in Mexico, summer rain can be seen falling, all at one time, on isolated patches of the landscape. This is selective rain, wetting the chapel in one village, the train station in another, a long empty stretch of highway in another. When these contained showers are distinguished against the mesas, people say, "It is raining in sleeves." A sleeve for Jesús María, a sleeve for Guadalupe de Atlas, a sleeve for every village and farm, if there is any sort of order at all under the skies.

Lately my memory, like those storms in Mexico, has begun to rain on me in sleeves. Today, writing at my desk on a March afternoon in California, I am deluged, without warning, by the contents of such a sleeve. All the houses I've ever lived in are raining down on me.

Three of them, destined to be objects of lifelong passion, were places that I knew by touch. My childhood sleeping porch, for instance. Long and narrow, it had been built onto the exterior of our house as the number of children multiplied from one to eight. Three cots, set head to foot in single file, entirely filled the porch. At the far end slept my oldest sister, Liz, at her feet the next oldest, Margaret, and finally, third in line, came my bed, with me in it and my hand against the redwood shingles.

Now, falling from memory's sleeve are three small girls with only a wire screen between them and wind, hail, new moons, and shooting stars. They breathe in the dark and cold, bound by blankets to hard mattresses, a chamber pot beneath each bed.

But why the hand on the shingled wall? Even now, seventy-five years later and possessing at last the long view, I cannot say whether I touched the wood to claim the house, to establish a connection, or simply for the sake of the shingles themselves, to feel their texture, to smell forest. I can resurrect them at will. I touch and smell them now.

Below the sleeping porch lay a garden, the nighttime province of gophers, frogs, and an occasional skunk. But when Liz was seventeen and had a party, Margaret and I watched shadows cross the lawn and listened to stifled laughter, urgent whispers, and an occasional silence so intense we almost heard it.

"They're necking," said Margaret, and together, two unseen, uncensorious witnesses, we moved closer to the screen.

For a better view, we looked down from the banister at the top of the stairs onto the heads and shoulders of dancing couples. "Moonlight on the Ganges" played a trio of piano, saxophone, and drums. "It Had to Be You." Boys we knew, pretending adulthood in starched wing collars and black bow ties, gathered at the living room door.

"Stags," said Margaret, and we gazed as, dancing in and out of the arms of these boys, girls drifted in pale chiffon with artificial flowers at the hip.

Margaret pointed to Allie Riggs and Babs Perth, two of Liz's friends observed through the wide threshold to be sitting on a sofa just inside.

"Wallflowers," said Margaret.

A few boys brought flasks and, at the height of the party, disappeared at intervals into the garden shrubbery.

Margaret said, "Bootleg," and we continued to peer down as dancing couples began to Charleston. The band played "Ain't She Sweet?"

And here today, on this spring afternoon, now might as well be then. The old songs are raining on me from the sleeve.

Come to me, my melancholy baby, I can't give you anything but love, You were meant for me, I cried for you, Thou swell, I'll get by, Side by side, Someone to watch over me, From Monday on, Always.

After Liz, the rest of us grew up and, one by one, had parties of our own. Eventually, all four daughters of the family married husbands in the room where they had danced.

The living room had a wide fireplace, a piano much practiced on, a wall of books, and a reproduction of the Winged Victory of Samothrace in front of a window at one end. I could come here after school, bring ginger ale and graham crackers, fold myself into a chair, and, undisturbed, read *Missing* by Mrs. Humphry Ward, *Graustark*, or *Les Misérables* for hours among my crumbs.

Directly overhead was my mother's room. Here she slept in the bed where five of her children were born and where, when the youngest was one, my father died.

Down the hall in a nursery turned schoolroom was the scarred round table where, chronologically, we learned to read and write. Our teacher, Miss Harriet Hannah Hutchins, traveled ten miles each way on the streetcar to fill our minds with words and numbers and how to find Vesuvius on a map.

Miss Hutchins' skirts swept the floor, failing to conceal a pronounced limp. She wore a garnet ring on her engagement finger, a gold watch on a chain, and in the sun a black straw hat secured to her head by jet pins. The limp, we found out, was the result of a fall from a horse when she was sixteen. The ring was not explained, but all of us assumed that she had once been engaged to a soldier or sailor killed in a war.

From time to time we visited the Hutchins family, who lived

among lemon trees in a white Victorian cottage with a front porch crowded with potted ferns and wicker chairs. In one of these, a rocker, sat Miss Hutchins' mother, an old woman so small-boned, thin-haired, and creased it seemed impossible that even the country air, even smelling as it did of lemon blossoms, could sustain her. Beside her, in a straight chair, sat Miss Frances, Miss Hutchins' younger sister, so gentle and obviously so good that we sensed she too, if only by her virtue, was somehow soon to perish.

In a corral across the drive, in the flickering shade of a mulberry tree, rested Miss Hutchins' aging horse, Alec, whom we fed lumps of sugar from flat palms. Then, under the gaze of old Mrs. Hutchins and Miss Frances, we picked handfuls of mulberry leaves to feed the silkworms about to spin themselves into cocoons on the schoolroom shelf.

Once Miss Hutchins invited me to visit her father's grave. We drove to the cemetery in a buggy behind Alec. I held snapdragons and larkspur, and she held the reins. It was a peaceful afternoon. I remember the clop of Alec's hooves, the fragrant groves on each side of us, and the high yellow sun above.

Arrived at the cemetery, we observed a moment's silence, while we stood on the grass beside a grave.

"My father lived to be eighty-nine," Miss Hutchins said. "He fought for the Union."

Familiar images gathered. Eliza on the ice. Lincoln at Gettysburg. General Lee and Traveler.

Then we drove back to the cottage in the absolute center of the same extraordinary peace.

Besides the silkworms, a hummingbird's nest with an egg in it and a stuffed wren were on display in the schoolroom. We found the nest one spring and, six months later, the expired bird, feet-up on a gravel path. Without wasting a second, Miss Hutchins had wrapped it in her handkerchief and carried it to the schoolroom table, where she gutted and repacked it before our astonished eyes.

But what was the stuffing? Sand, grain, dry bread, or simple cotton batting? Did she sew up the feathered breast with darning thread? I saw the bird dead on the path. I saw it stuffed, its beak closed, its claws uncurled, perched on the bookcase. I believe I witnessed the reincarnation. But no matter. All of it, what I saw and what I didn't, is now the blood and bone of memory.

In the schoolroom during World War I we knitted balls of wool into ragged squares to help the American soldiers. When there were enough of these, they were collected to be sewn into blankets. And what odd blankets they must have been, knitted and purled by half-grown hands out of skeins of favorite colors.

Once you could make a square without dropping stitches, you could go on to mufflers. One day a letter came from an American soldier in France, thanking me for a muffler. I kept the yellowing pages for fifty years, through various changes of address and turnings-out of closets, until finally, once and for all, it disappeared.

Miss Hutchins' era ended, and we grew out of braces and into poetry. Often, without warning, Margaret, in her middy blouse and serge skirt, would fling open my door as I did homework and cry, "I have a rendezvous with Death at some disputed barricade," or "If I should die, think only this of me . . ."

She knew all the repetitive poems by heart: "Boots, boots, boots, boots," "The highwayman came riding, riding, riding," and "Go down to Kew in lilac time, in lilac time, in lilac time."

On the evening of the day she bobbed her hair, she struck my door open and called out, "What lips my lips have kissed, and where, and why, I have forgotten," going on with scarcely a pause to "Last night, ah, yesternight, betwixt her lips and mine there fell thy shadow, Cynara, and the night was thine." And we were both impaled on the words.

Outside the room where these performances took place stretched the sleeping porch. From where I sat, dipping my pen into ink, I had only to take two steps and reach through a window to touch the redwood shingles, feel their rough grain.

Beyond the porch and the lawn, entirely separated from care and cultivation by an evergreen hedge, sloped a wild hillside of oaks, eucalyptus, weeds, and matilija poppies, whose crushed tissue-paper petals unfolded every June into white flowers as big as a child's face.

Halfway down this hill an ancient acacia, which still produced a few yellow clusters in spring, supported a tree house, consisting of two platforms of pine boards. Its lack of a roof and walls failed to diminish our pleasure in it. Here we played and quarreled and took up candy bars to eat.

Sometimes I had the tree house to myself. Then I would sit cross-legged on the top floor and watch the afternoon turn into night. I realize now that these were my only chances, alone in the tree house, to ache. Without interruption or observers, to ache for the world, and for me in it.

I had left the house where I was born and had a husband and child when Miss Hutchins was brought down by cancer. I took some late roses and a few spikes of lavender to the hospital, and she tried to notice them. She was too tired to speak. It was only when I stood up to go that Miss Hutchins said, in a voice I hardly knew, "The pain is unendurable. I cannot stand the pain." Then added, "I have talked to the doctor." She died eleven days, or two hundred and sixty-four hours, later.

Now all the other houses are raining from the sleeve.

First is an old California adobe my husband and I and our small children lived in for five years. Built in 1816 as a grist mill for a Franciscan mission, it had already been named a historic monument when we moved in. Surviving age, earthquakes, and damage by occupants, the mill stood solid and pristine in a revised neighborhood. A nearby lake had long since been drained, the surrounding fields and groves turned suburb. But the old building, its original acre, inside its high outer wall, was immune to change, out of context and out of time.

"How is it to come in from the street and step through the gate in your wall?" people asked us.

And we said, "Magic."

For it was all enchanted. The high beams tied with leather thongs, the windows set in walls four feet thick, the whitewashed interior, the border that took the place of baseboards, painted with vegetable colors in an Indian design.

The old mill absorbed anachronisms. No matter that my first typewriter occupied a table in a bedroom or that a model airplane hung from a sycamore tree. No difference the diapers drying in front of the living room fire or the tricycle in the patio. If Junípero Serra himself had walked in, he would only have had to touch the walls to know that he was home.

The garden claimed a few witnesses from the past—a bent black walnut tree, a gnarled olive, and a Castilian rose. Filling up the space around them, orange trees flowered and bore fruit, the red blossoms of a hedge turned into a hundred pomegranates in the fall, and a dozen plants that looked like giant thistles produced long-stemmed artichokes.

On weekend mornings in the old mill, we were often roused from sleep by the arrival outside of unexpected visitors. Some of them came only to look and, if the light was right, take pictures. Others came to work. From our bedroom my husband and I, still in pajamas and nightgown, would gaze down on painters, settled on stools before their easels, or on persons carrying maps who scientifically paced the ground between the walls. These were treasure hunters, searching for Spanish gold.

"The Franciscan fathers are known to have buried it here," they told us, but the distances on the maps never corresponded to the dimensions of the garden.

Once an elderly man made himself at home with a divining rod and for two April days moved slowly between tree and path, grapevine and agave.

"It's got to be here somewhere," he said.

"Is it in doubloons?" we asked, and he nodded.

He left empty-handed, but we agreed with him. It had to be there somewhere.

In the bedroom that used to be a granary I composed a number of poems that rhymed, usually in quatrains, and submitted them to magazines. These, not surprisingly and without exception, failed. Fifty years later I still have the printed rejections. Unlike the handwritten note from the soldier of World War I, they were never lost.

It was from this house, when I was twenty-five, that I first traveled into the interior of Mexico. Not just to a border town, as previously, but to the heart of the country, Mexico City, three days and nights by train behind a steam locomotive.

We stayed in a post-colonial house a block from the Paseo de la Reforma, between the *glorietas* of Diana and the Angel. In the center of one, the goddess of the hunt, circled by traffic, lifted her bow and arrow over thirty mongrels lapping at the basin below. In the second, from the top of a soaring column, a golden angel raised a laurel wreath over buses, trucks, carts, and sidewalks crowded with vendors, beggars, pedestrians, and petty thieves.

The house of our relatives was dark, high-ceilinged, and, except at midday, cold. During a week's visit, I was never allowed to enter the kitchen, where a barefoot, loose-braided family retainer named María de Jesús kept a parrot on a perch above the stove, occasionally encouraging it to fly. Old, gold-toothed, homesick for the distant place where she was born, she survived by re-creating it among the alien pots and pans.

On this first trip to Mexico, I went to an Aztec pyramid, to the canals on whose banks flowers are grown, to the opera house, which sinks lower a fraction of an inch each day, and to a nightclub. I see now that in this week I failed utterly to penetrate the surface of Mexico. But was it then that the spell fell on me?

I have lived most of fifty years in the California hillside house where I write today. But in spite of its long history of Christmases and birthdays, measles and chicken pox, music lessons and menageries, I have little to say of it. As long as I continue to inhabit it, how am I to see it plain and clear? We are not through with each other, this house and I.

When we had lived here nine years, we rented its wisteria vine and windows with views to a safe tenant and moved to a house with a crimson door in Mexico City. This house backed into a hill and had adjacent structures on both sides, so that all its rooms faced front.

To enter, you opened a narrow red door next to a wide red one that closed the garage. Then you continued along a red passageway toward a glass aviary on an upper level. This birdcage served as the fourth and outside wall of the red dining room, which lay directly behind.

And now, out of memory's sleeve, falls a shower of birds. For in this cage lived crested cardinals, perching listlessly on defoliated twigs or pecking for seeds mixed with gravel on the aviary floor.

While we ate our egg sandwich, or chop, in the blood-red dining room, we gazed at the matching birds. Sometimes one of us rose from the table and tapped on the glass to remind the cardinals that we, too, swam in this crimson sea.

At the end of the first week, we visited a specialist at the pet store.

"Cardenales," he said, and fell silent. Then he said, "They are molting," and we said, "Yes."

"They have light," he said, and we said, "No," and explained that although the aviary faced the street, a pepper tree had grown between it and the sun.

"Caray!" the man said, contracting *"Caramba,"* and sold us food supplements of vitamin D.

The next day we asked our landlady to remove the cardinals.

"They are better off in the aviary," she said. "Outside, they would be pecked to death by other birds."

Was it one or was it two cardinals that died of chronic deprivation during our year's tenancy? And did we replace them when we left, as we did a few glasses and a cup? But by that time, the whole situation had changed. For as the cardinals declined above, field mice began to enter through a hole in the aviary floor and forage for fallen seed. Even rounder and tamer than the creations of Potter and Disney, the fattening mice somehow compensated for the daily worsening of the birds.

Our dinner guests, entranced, ate with eyes fixed on the glass cage. Like visitors to a zoo, they pondered the mice and the birds. They asked to be invited back.

The house with the red door had a flat roof, where clothes were washed and hung to dry. On the roof, which was 7,500 feet above sea level, the air was like sea air, light and crisp. If not for the hill behind the house, we could have stood there, looked over the city, its parks, palaces, and slums, and beyond, over farms, fields, and Indian ruins, all the way to the volcanos, Popo and Ixti, the two lovers under the snow.

Years later we took possession of the second white adobe in our lives. This one was in central Mexico, a day's drive from the capital, at the edge of a village of little water and few trees, a place whose inhabitants burned and shivered according to the season within a circle of barren hills. But not barren at all, of course, if you count rocks and their formations. Almost as soon as we arrived, trucks started bringing loads of these rocks to our house, for a wall, for a border, for some steps. When the mason split them, they broke in halves of all shades of rose and green and sand. Some had blue streaks. Some were specked with gold. Each was as individual as a piece of jade. You knew them best by touching them, by moving along the half-finished wall, your hand sliding from one rough surface to the next. Dry, hard, complex, indifferent, they were the fiber of our world.

"How old are they?" you might ask.

"Ay, quién sabe?" the mason said. "As old as all of it," and he would wave an arm from one horizon to another, encompassing mountains, fields, cows, goats, a church dome, the hoist tower of an idle mine, geraniums in a pot, a lizard on a tile. He had no thought of millenniums of fire and ice, of convulsions at the planet's core. The mason only meant the rocks were as old as the day when the whole idea occurred to God.

The true sound of Mexico is not the braying of the burro or the baying of the coyote, nor is it the plaint of the beggar or the passion in a song. The true, infallible, recognizable sound is the pounding of the mason's chisel against stone.

Our early mornings in this place were all alike. We woke in our square, beam-ceilinged room first to sunrise, then, in this order, to cockcrow, church bell, birdsong, and the rhythmic chipping away of stone. We bathed and brushed our teeth to the sound of it, spoke and ate to it.

We met the mason on our first day in the village. Twenty-five years later, when I left for the last time, his son, a master of the same craft, stood in the driveway to see me off. He was one of a small crowd that had gathered. When the last things, my thermos and my sandwich, were in the car, I shook hands with each one—the watchman, his daughter and grandson, the cook, the carpenter, the electrician-mechanic turned majordomo, the boy who gardened, and the man who every spring borrowed our empty field to plant his corn.

When I looked back from the gate, they were all still there, and I almost stopped to lean out and wave again.

But such a thing was impossible. They would have thought I had forgotten something and come after me to help.

I would have had to say, "Oh, no, I've left nothing behind," and thank them again. I would have said, "See for yourselves. It is all here," and, for the second time, left it all behind.

Eventually some Mexican stones found their way to my California garden. Geodes sometimes appear when ivy is cut back. A rock that was once the color of amethyst has taken a permanent place under an orange tree. Birds drink from a shell carved from *cantera,* the marble of Mexico.

"Do you want to keep these rocks?" asks the gardener, whose

mother as a child fled a village not far from ours during the revolution of 1910. He looks at half a dozen ore samples, some still showing copper, some still showing lead, scattered without purpose along a brick border.

And I say, "Yes. Keep them," knowing that as soon as his back is turned, I will take one up and immediately enter that other garden two thousand miles to the south. It is noon and hot. I can pick the first ripe fig. I can touch the first hard-fought-for rose.

From the desk where I write today, I face a window three-quarters full of sky. At my left hand is a chip of copper ore that shows azurite. For no other reasons than these, I see all at once that everything is possible. I have recovered my houses. Now I can bring back the rest, picnics and circuses, train rides and steamers, labels on trunks, and wreaths for the dead on front doors.

I have everything I need. A square of sky, a piece of stone, a page, a pen, and memory raining down on me in sleeves.

Part V

Edie: A Life

Edie: A Life

In the middle of an April night in 1919, a plain woman named Edith Fisk, lifted from England to California on a tide of world peace, arrived at the Ransom house to raise five half-orphaned children.

A few hours later, at seven in the morning, this Edith, more widely called Edie, invited the three eldest to her room for tea. They were James, seven; Eliza, six; and Jenny, four. Being handed cups of tea, no matter how reduced by milk, made them believe that they had grown up overnight.

"Have some sugar," said Edie, and spooned it in. Moments

later she said, "Have another cup." But her *h*'s went unspoken and became the first of hundreds, then thousands, that would accumulate in the corners of the house and thicken in the air like sighs.

In an adjoining room the twins, entirely responsible for their mother's death, had finished their bottles and fallen back into guiltless sleep. At the far end of the house, the widower, Thomas Ransom, who had spent the night aching for his truant wife, lay across his bed, half awake, half asleep, and dreaming.

The three children sat in silence at Edie's table. She had grizzled hair pulled up in a knot, heavy brows, high cheeks, and two long hairs in her chin. She was bony and flat and looked starched, like the apron she had tied around her. Her teeth were large and white and even, her eyes an uncompromising blue.

She talked to the children as if they were her age, forty-one. "My father was an ostler," she told them, and they listened without comprehension. "My youngest brother died at Wipers," she said. "My nephew was gassed at Verdun."

These were places the children had never heard of. But all three of them, even Jenny, understood the word "died."

"Our mother died," said James.

Edie nodded.

"I was born, the oldest of eight, in Atherleigh, a town in Devon. I've lived in five English counties," she told them, without saying what a county was. "And taken care of thirty children, a few of them best forgotten."

"Which ones?" said James.

But Edie talked only of her latest charges, the girls she had left to come to America.

"Lady Alice and Lady Anne," said Edie, and described two paragons of quietness and clean knees, who lived in a castle in Kent.

Edie didn't say "castle," she said "big brick house." She didn't say "lake," she said "pond." But the children, dazzled by illustrations in Cinderella and King Arthur, assumed princesses. And after that, they assumed castle, tower, moat, lake, lily, swan.

Lady Alice was seven and Lady Anne was eight when last seen immaculately crayoning with their ankles crossed in the tower overlooking the lake.

Eliza touched Edie's arm. "What is gassed?" she said.

Edie explained.

Jenny lifted her spoon for attention. "I saw Father cry," she said. "Twice."

"Oh, be quiet," said James.

With Edie, they could say anything.

After that morning, they would love tea forever, all their lives, in sitting rooms and restaurants, on terraces and balconies, at sidewalk cafés and whistle stops, even under awnings in the rain. They would drink it indiscriminately, careless of flavor, out of paper cups or Spode, with lemon, honey, milk, or cream, with spices or with rum.

Before Edie came to the Ransom house, signs of orphanhood were everywhere—in the twins' colic, in Eliza's aggravated impulse to pinch Jenny, in the state of James's sheets every morning. Their father, recognizing symptoms of grief, brought home wrapped packages in his overcoat pockets. He gave the children a Victrola and Harry Lauder records.

"Shall we read?" he would ask in the evening, and take Edward Lear from the shelf. " 'There was an Old Man with a beard,' " read Thomas Ransom, and he and his children listened solemnly to the unaccustomed voice speaking the familiar words.

While the twins baffled everyone by episodes of weight loss and angry tears, various efforts to please were directed toward the other three. The cook baked cakes and frosted their names into the icing. The sympathetic gardener packed them into his wheelbarrow and pushed them at high speeds down sloping paths. Two aunts, the dead mother's sisters, improvised weekly outings—to the ostrich farm, the alligator farm, the lion farm, to a picnic in the mountains, a shell hunt at the beach. These contrived entertainments failed. None substituted for what was needed: the reappearance at the piano or on the stairs of a young woman with freckles, green eyes, and a ribbon around her waist.

Edie came to the rescue of the Ransoms through the intervention of the aunts' English friend, Cissy. When hope for joy in any degree was almost lost, Cissy wrote and produced the remedy.

The aunts brought her letter to Thomas Ransom in his study on a February afternoon. Outside the window, a young sycamore, planted by his wife the year before, cast its sparse shadow on a patch of grass.

Cissy wrote that all her friends lost sons and brothers in the war and she was happy she had none to offer up. Wherever one went in London, wounded veterans, wearing their military medals, were performing for money. She saw a legless man in uniform playing an accordion outside Harrods. Others, on Piccadilly, had harmonicas wired in front of their faces so they could play without hands. Blind men, dressed for parade, sang in the rain for theater queues.

And the weather, wrote Cissy. Winter seemed to be a state of life and not a season. How lucky one was to be living, untouched by it all, in America, particularly California. Oh, to wake up to sunshine every morning, to spend one's days warm and dry.

Now she arrived at the point of her letter. Did anyone they knew want Edith Fisk, who had taken care of children for twenty-five years and was personally known to Cissy? Edie intended to live near a cousin in Texas. California might be just the place.

The reading of the letter ended.

"Who is Cissy?" said Thomas Ransom, unable to foresee that within a dozen years he would marry her.

James, who had been listening at the door, heard only the first part of the letter. Long before Cissy proposed Edie, he was upstairs in his room, trying to attach a harmonica to his mouth with kite string.

Edie was there within two months. The aunts and Thomas Ransom began to witness change.

Within weeks the teasing stopped. Within months the nighttime sheets stayed dry. The twins, male and identical, fattened and pulled toys apart. Edie bestowed on each of the five children equal shares of attention and concern. She hung their drawings in her room, even the ones of moles in traps and inhabited houses burning to the ground. Samples of the twins' scribblings remained on permanent display. The children's pictures eventually occupied almost all one wall and surrounded a framed photograph of Lady Alice and Lady Anne, two small light-haired girls sitting straight-backed on dappled ponies.

"Can we have ponies?" Eliza and Jenny asked their father. But he had fallen in love with a woman named Trish and, distracted, brought home a cage of canaries instead.

Edie and the Ransom children suited each other. It seemed right to them all that she had come to braid hair, turn hems,

push swings, take walks; to apply iodine to cuts and embrace the
cry that followed, to pinch her fingers between the muddy rubber
and the shoe. Edie stopped nightmares almost before they
started. At a child's first gasp she would be in the doorway, uncombed and minus her false teeth, tying on her wrapper, a glass
of water in her hand.

The older children repaid this bounty with torments of their
own devising. They would rush at her in a trio, shout, "We've
'idden your 'at in the 'all," and run shrieking with laughter, out
of her sight. They crept into her room at night, found the pink
gums and big white teeth where they lay floating in a mug, and,
in a frenzy of bad manners, hid them in a hatbox or behind the
books.

Edie never reported these lapses of deportment to Thomas
Ransom. Instead, she would invoke the names and virtues of
Lady Alice and Lady Anne.

"They didn't talk like roustabouts," said Edie. "They slept
like angels through the night."

Between spring and fall the nonsense ceased. Edie grew into
the Ransoms' lives and was accepted there, like air and water and
the food they ate. From the start, the children saw her as a refuge.
Flounder as they might in the choppy sea where orphans and
half-orphans drown, they trusted her to save them.

Later on, when their father emerged from mourning, Edie was
the mast they clung to in a squall of stepmothers.

Within a period of twelve years Thomas Ransom, grasping at

the outer fringe of happiness, brought three wives in close succession to the matrimonial bed he first shared with the children's now sainted mother. He chose women he believed were like her, and it was true that all three, Trish, Irene, and Cissy, were small-boned and energetic. But they were brown-eyed and, on the whole, not musical.

The first to come was Trish, nineteen years old and porcelain-skinned. Before her arrival Thomas Ransom asked the children not to come knocking at his bedroom door day and night, as they had in the past. Once she was there, other things changed. The children heard him humming at his desk in the study. They noticed that he often left in midmorning, instead of at eight, for the office where he practiced law.

Eliza asked questions at early-morning tea. "Why are they always in their room, with the door locked?"

And Jenny said, "Yes. Even before dinner."

"Don't you know anything?" said James.

Edie poured more pale tea. "Hold your cups properly. Don't spill," she told them, and the lost *h* floated into the steam rising from the pot.

Trish, at nineteen, was neither mother nor sister to the children. Given their priorities of blood and birth and previous residence, they inevitably outdistanced her. They knew to the oldest steamer trunk and the latest cookie the contents of the attic and larder.

They walked oblivious across rugs stained with their spilled ink. The hall banister shone with the years of their sliding. Long ago they had enlisted the cook and the gardener as allies. Three of them remembered their mother. The other two thought they did.

Trish said good morning at noon and drove off with friends. Later she paused to say good night in a rustle of taffeta on Thomas Ransom's arm as they left for a dinner or a dance.

James made computations. "She's nine years older than I am," he said, "and eighteen years younger than Father."

"He keeps staring at her," said Eliza.

"And kissing her hand," said Jenny.

Edie opened a door on a sliver of her past. "I knew a girl once with curly red hair like that, in Atherleigh."

"What was her name?" James asked, as if for solid evidence.

Edie bit off her darning thread. She looked backward with her inward eye. Finally she said, "Lily Stiles. The day I went into service in Dorset, Lily went to work at the Rose and Plough."

"The Rose and Plough," repeated Eliza. "What's that?"

"It's a pub," said Edie, and she explained what a public house was. Immediately, this establishment, with its gleaming bar and its game of darts, was elevated in the children's minds to the mysterious realm of Lady Alice and Lady Anne and set in place a stone's throw from their castle.

At home, Trish's encounters with her husband's children were brief. In passing, she waved to them all and patted the twins on their dark heads. She saw more of the three eldest on those Saturday afternoons when she took them, along with Edie, to the movies.

Together they sat in the close, expectant dark of the Rivoli Theater, watched the shimmering curtains part, shivered to the organist's opening chords, and, at the appearance of an image on the screen, cast off their everyday lives to be periled, rescued, rejected, and adored. They sat spellbound through the film and when the words "The End" came on, rose depleted and blinking from their seats to face the hot sidewalk and full sun outside.

Trish selected the pictures, and though they occasionally included Fairbanks films and ones that starred the Gishes, these were not her favorites. She detested comedies. To avoid Harold Lloyd, they saw Rudolph Valentino in *The Sheik*. Rather than endure Buster Keaton, they went to *Camille*, starring Alla Nazimova.

"I should speak to your father," Edie would say later on at home. But she never did. Instead, she only remarked at bedtime, "It's a nice change, going to the pictures."

Trish left at the end of two years, during which the children, according to individual predispositions, grew taller and developed the hands and feet and faces they would always keep. They learned more about words and numbers, they began to like oysters, they swam the Australian crawl. They survived crises. These included scarlet fever, which the twins contracted and recovered from, and James's near electrocution as a result of his tinkering with wires and sockets.

Eliza and Jenny, exposed to chicken pox on the same day, ran simultaneous fevers and began to scratch. Edie brought ice and invented games. She cleared the table between their beds and knotted a handkerchief into arms and legs and a smooth, round head. She made it face each invalid and bow.

"This is how my sister Frahnces likes to dahnce the fahncy dahnces," Edie said, and the knotted handkerchief waltzed and two-stepped back and forth across the table.

Mesmerized by each other, the twins made few demands. A mechanical walking bear occupied them for weeks, a wind-up train for months. They shared a rocking horse and crashed slowly into one another on tricycles.

James, at eleven, sat in headphones by the hour in front of a crystal radio set. Sometimes he invited Edie to scratch a chip of rock with wire and hear a human voice advance and recede in the distance.

"Where's he talking from?" Edie would ask, and James said, "Oak Bluff. Ten miles away."

Together they marveled.

The two aunts, after one of their frequent visits, tried to squeeze the children into categories. James is the experimenter, they agreed. Jenny, the romantic. The twins, at five, too young to pigeonhole. Eliza was the bookish one.

A single-minded child, she read while walking to school, in the car on mountain curves, on the train in tunnels, on her back on the beach at noon, in theaters under dimming lights, between the sheets by flashlight. Eliza saw all the world through thick lenses adjusted for fine print. On Saturdays, she would often desert her invited friend and choose to read by herself instead.

At these times Edie would approach the bewildered visitor. Would she like to feed the canaries? Climb into the tree house?

"We'll make tiaras," she told one abandoned guest and, taking Jenny along, led the way to the orange grove.

"We're brides," announced Jenny a few minutes later, and she and Eliza's friend, balancing circles of flowers on their heads, stalked in a barefoot procession of two through the trees.

That afternoon, Jenny, as though she had never seen it before, inquired about Edie's ring. "Are you engaged?"

"I was once," said Edie, and went on to expose another slit of her past. "To Alfred Trotter."

"Was he killed at Wipers?"

Edie shook her head. "The war came later. He worked for his father at the Rose and Plough."

In a field beyond the grove, Jenny saw a plough, ploughing roses.

"Why didn't you get married?"

Edie looked at her watch and said it was five o'clock. She brushed off her skirt and got to her feet. "I wasn't the only girl in Atherleigh."

Jenny, peering into the past, caught a glimpse of Lily Stiles behind the bar at the Rose and Plough.

After Trish left, two more years went by before the children's father brought home his third wife. This was Irene, come to transplant herself in Ransom ground. Behind her she trailed a wake of friends, men with beards and women in batik scarves, who sat about the porch with big hats between them and the sun. In a circle of wicker chairs, they discussed Cubism, Freud, Proust, and Schoenberg's twelve-tone row. They passed perfumed candies to the children.

Irene changed all the lampshades in the house from white paper to red silk, threw a Persian prayer rug over the piano, and gave the children incense sticks for Christmas. She recited poems translated from the Sanskrit and wore saris to the grocery store. In spite of efforts on both sides, Irene remained an envoy from a foreign land.

One autumn day, not long before the end of her tenure as Thomas Ransom's wife, she took Edie and all five children to a fortune-teller at the county fair. A pale-eyed, wasted man sold them tickets outside Madame Zelma's tent and pointed to the curtained entrance. Crowding into the stale air of the interior, they gradually made out the fortune-teller's veiled head and jeweled neck behind two lighted candelabra on a desk.

"Have a seat," said Madame.

All found places on a bench or on hassocks, and rose, one by one, to approach the palmist as she beckoned them to a chair facing her.

Madame Zelma, starting with the eldest, pointed to Edie.

"I see children," said the fortune-teller. She concentrated in silence for a moment. "You will cross the ocean. I see a handsome man."

Us, thought Jenny. Alfred Trotter.

Madame Zelma, having wound Edie's life backward from present to past, summoned Irene.

"I see a musical instrument," said Madame, as if she knew of Irene's guitar and the chords in minor keys that were its repertory. "Your flower is the poppy. Your fruit, the pear." The fortune-teller leaned closer to Irene's hand. "Expect a change of residence soon."

Edie and the children listened.

And so the fortunes went, the three eldest children's full of prizes and professions, talents and awards, happy marriages, big families, silver mines, and fame.

By the time Madame Zelma reached the twins, she had little left to predict. "Long lives," was all she told them. But what more could anyone divine from the trackless palms of seven-year-olds?

By the time Cissy, the next wife, came, James's voice had changed and his sisters had bobbed their hair. The twins had joined in painting an oversized panorama titled "After the Earthquake." Edie hung it on her wall.

Cissy, the children's last stepmother, traveled all the way from England, like Edie. Introduced by the aunts through a letter, Thomas Ransom met her in London, rode with her in Hyde Park, drove with her to Windsor for the day, then took her boating on the upper reaches of the Thames. They were married in a registry, she for the third time, he for the fourth, and spent their honeymoon on the Isle of Skye in a long, gray drizzle.

"I can hardly wait for California," said Cissy.

Once there, she lay about in the sun until she blistered. "Darling, bring my parasol, bring my gloves," she entreated whichever child was near.

"Are the hills always this brown?" she asked, splashing rose water on her throat. "Has that stream dried up for good?"

Cissy climbed mountain paths looking for wildflowers and came back with toyon and sage. Twice a week on her horse, Sweet William, she rode trails into the countryside, flushing up rattlesnakes instead of grouse.

On national holidays that celebrated American separation from Britain, Cissy felt some way historically at fault. On the day before Thanksgiving, she strung cranberries silently at Edie's side. On the Fourth of July they sat together holding sparklers six thousand miles from the counties where their roots, still green, were sunk in English soil.

During the dry season of the year, from April to December, the children sometimes watched Cissy as she stood at a corner of the terrace, her head turning from east to west, her eyes searching the implacable blue sky. But for what? An English bird? The smell of fog?

By now the children were half grown or more, and old enough to recognize utter misery.

"Cissy didn't know what to expect," they told each other.

"She's homesick for the Sussex Downs," said Edie, releasing the *h* into space.

"Are you homesick too, for Atherleigh?" asked Eliza.

"I am not."

"You knew what to expect," said Jenny.

Edie said, "Almost."

The children discussed with her the final departure of each stepmother.

"Well, she's gone," said James, who was usually called to help carry out bags. "Maybe we'll have some peace."

After Cissy left, he made calculations. "Between the three of them, they had six husbands," he told the others.

"And Father's had four wives," said one of the twins. "Six husbands and four wives make ten," said the other.

"Ten what?" said James.

"Poor souls," said Edie.

🌿

At last the children were as tall as they would ever be. The aunts could no longer say, "How are they ever to grow up?" For here they were, reasonably bright and reasonably healthy, survivors of a world war and a great depression, durable relics of their mother's premature and irreversible defection and their father's abrupt marriages.

They had got through it all—the removal of tonsils, the straightening of teeth, the first night at camp, the first dance, the goodbyes waved from the rear platforms of trains that, like boats crossing the Styx, carried them away to college. This is not to say they were the same children they would have been if their mother had lived. They were not among the few who can suffer anything, loss or gain, without effect. But no one could point to a Ransom child's smile or frown or sleeping habits and reasonably comment, "No mother."

Edie stayed in the Ransom house until the twins left for college. By now, Eliza and Jenny were married, James married, divorced, and remarried. Edie went to all the graduations and weddings.

On these occasions the children hurried across playing fields and lawns to reach and embrace her.

"Edie!" they said. "You came!" They introduced their fellow graduates and the persons they had married. "This is Edie. Edie, this is Bill, Terry, Peter, Joan," and they were carried off in whirlwinds of friends.

As the Ransom house emptied of family, it began to expand. The bedrooms grew larger, the hall banister longer, the porch too wide for the wicker chairs. Edie took leave of the place for want of children in 1938. She was sixty years old.

She talked to Thomas Ransom in his study, where his first wife's portrait, painted in pastels, had been restored to its place on the wall facing his desk. Edie sat under the green-eyed young face, her unfaltering blue glance on her employer. Each tried to make the parting easy. It was clear, however, that they were dividing between them, top to bottom, a frail, towering structure of nineteen accumulated years, which was the time it had taken to turn five children, with their interminable questions, unfounded terrors, and destructive impulses, into mature adults who could vote, follow maps, make omelets, and reach an accord of sorts with life and death.

Thinking back over the intervening years, Thomas Ransom remembered Edie's cousin in Texas and inquired, only to find that Texas had been a disappointment, as had America itself. The cousin had returned to England twelve years ago.

"Would you like that?" he asked Edie. "To go back to England?"

She had grown used to California, she said. She had no one in Atherleigh. So in the end, prompted by the look in his first wife's eyes, Thomas Ransom offered Edie a cottage and a pension, to be hers for the rest of her life.

❦

Edie's beach cottage was two blocks back from the sea and very small. On one wall she hung a few of the children's drawings, including the earthquake aftermath. Opposite them, by itself, she hung the framed photograph of Lady Alice and Lady Anne, fair and well-seated astride their ponies. Edie had become the repository of pets. The long-lived fish swam languidly in one corner of her sitting room, the last of the canaries molted in another.

Each Ransom child came to her house once for tea, pulling in to the curb next to a mailbox marked Edith Fisk.

"Edie, you live so far away!"

On their first Christmas apart, the children sent five cards, the next year four, then two for several years, then one, or sometimes none.

During the first September of Edie's retirement, England declared war on Germany. She knitted socks for the British troops, and on one occasion four years after she left it, returned briefly to the Ransom house. This was when the twins were killed in Europe a month apart, at the age of twenty-four, one in a fighter plane over the Baltic, the other in a bomber over the Rhine. Two months later Thomas Ransom asked Edie to dispose of their things, and she came back for a week to her old, now anonymous, room.

She was unprepared for the mass of articles to be dealt with.

The older children had cleared away childhood possessions at the time of their marriages. But here were all the books the twins had ever read, from Dr. Dolittle to Hemingway, and all their entertainments, from a Ouija board to skis and kites. Years of their civilian trousers, coats, and shoes crowded the closets.

Edie first wrapped and packed the bulky objects, then folded into cartons the heaps of clothing, much of which she knew. A week was barely time enough to sort it all and reach decisions. Then, suddenly, as though it had been a matter of minutes, the boxes were packed and at the door. Edie marked each one with black crayon. Boys Club, she printed, Children's Hospital, Red Cross, Veterans.

That afternoon she stood for a moment with Thomas Ransom on the porch, the silent house behind them. The November air was cold and fresh, the sky cloudless.

"Lovely day," said Edie.

Thomas Ransom nodded, admiring the climate while his life thinned out.

If the three surviving children had written Edie during the years that followed, this is what she would have learned.

At thirty-five, James, instead of having become an electrical engineer or a master mechanic, was a junior partner in his father's law firm. Twice divorced and about to take a new wife, he had apparently learned nothing from Thomas Ransom, not even how to marry happily once. Each marriage had produced two children, four intended cures that failed. James's practice involved foreign corporations, and he was often abroad. He moved from executive offices to boardrooms and back, and made no attempt to diagnose his discontent. On vacations at home, he dismantled and reassembled heaters and fans and wired every room of his house for sound.

Whenever he visited England, he tried, and failed, to find time to send Edie a card.

Eliza had been carried off from her research library by an archaeologist ten years older and three inches shorter than she. He took her first to Guatemala, then to Mexico, where they lived in a series of jungle huts in Chiapas and Yucatán. It was hard to find native help, and the clothes Eliza washed often hung drying for days on the teeming underbrush. Her damp books, on shelves and still in boxes, began to mildew. She cooked food wrapped in leaves over a charcoal fire. On special days, like her birthday and Christmas, Eliza would stand under the thatch of her doorway and stare northwest through the rain and vegetation in the direction of the house where she was born and had first tasted tea.

Edie was still living in the house when Jenny, through a letter from her last stepmother, Cissy, met the Englishman she would marry. Thin as a pencil and pale as parchment, he had entered the local university as an exchange fellow. Jenny was immediately moved to take care of him, sew on his missing buttons, comb his sandy hair. His English speech enchanted her.

"Tell about boating at Henley," she urged him. "Tell about climbing the Trossachs. Explain cricket." And while he described these things as fully as his inherent reserve would allow, the inflections of another voice fell across his. Jenny heard "fahncy dahnces." She heard "poor souls."

"Have you ever been to Atherleigh in Devon?" she asked him.

"That's Hatherleigh," he said.

If Jenny had written Edie, she would have said, "I love Massachusetts, I love my house, I can make scones, come and see us."

On a spring afternoon in 1948, Thomas Ransom called his children together in the same study where the aunts had read Cissy's letter of lament and recommendation. The tree his wife planted thirty years ago towered in green leaf outside the window.

The children had gathered from the outposts of the world—James from Paris, Eliza from the Mayan tropics, Jenny from snowed-in Boston. When he summoned them, they had assumed a crisis involving their father. Now they sat uneasily under the portrait of their mother, a girl years younger than themselves. Thomas Ransom offered them tea and sherry. He looked through the window at the tree.

At last he presented his news. "Edie is dying," he said. "She is in the hospital with cancer," as if cancer were a friend Edie had always longed to share a room with.

They visited her on a shining April morning, much like the one when they first met. With their first gray hairs and new lines at their eyes, they waited a moment on the hospital steps.

James took charge. "We'll go in one by one," he said.

So, as if they had rehearsed together, one after another they stood alone outside the door that had a sign, No Visitors, stood there while patients prepared for surgery or carts of half-eaten lunches were wheeled past, stood and collected their childhood until a nurse noticed and said, "Go in. She wants to see you." Then each one pushed the door open, went to the high narrow bed, and said, "Edie."

She may not have known they were there. She had started to be a skeleton. Her skull was pulling her eyes in. Once they had spoken her name, there was nothing more to say. Before leaving, they touched the familiar, unrecognizable hand of shoelaces and hair ribbons and knew it, for the first time, disengaged.

After their separate visits, they assembled again on the hospital steps. It was now they remembered Lady Alice and Lady Anne.

"Where was that castle?" Eliza asked.

"In Kent," said Jenny.

All at one time, they imagined the girls in their tower after tea. Below them, swans pulled lengthening reflections across the smooth surface of the lake. Lady Alice sat at her rosewood desk, Lady Anne at hers. They were still seven and eight years old. They wrote on thick paper with mother-of-pearl pens dipped into ivory inkwells.

"Dear Edie," wrote Lady Alice.

"Dear Edie," wrote Lady Anne.

"I am sorry to hear you are ill," they both wrote.

Then, as if they were performing an exercise in penmanship, they copied "I am sorry" over and over in flowing script until they reached the bottom of the page. When there was no more room, they signed one letter "Alice" and the other letter "Anne."

In the midst of all this, Edie died.

FOR THE BEST IN PAPERBACKS, LOOK FOR THE

In every corner of the world, on every subject under the sun, Penguin represents quality and variety—the very best in publishing today.

For complete information about books available from Penguin—including Puffins, Penguin Classics, and Arkana—and how to order them, write to us at the appropriate address below. Please note that for copyright reasons the selection of books varies from country to country.

In the United Kingdom: Please write to *Dept. JC, Penguin Books Ltd, FREEPOST, West Drayton, Middlesex UB7 0BR.*

If you have any difficulty in obtaining a title, please send your order with the correct money, plus ten percent for postage and packaging, to *P.O. Box No. 11, West Drayton, Middlesex UB7 0BR*

In the United States: Please write to *Consumer Sales, Penguin USA, P.O. Box 999, Dept. 17109, Bergenfield, New Jersey 07621-0120.* VISA and MasterCard holders call 1-800-253-6476 to order all Penguin titles

In Canada: Please write to *Penguin Books Canada Ltd, 10 Alcorn Avenue, Suite 300, Toronto, Ontario M4V 3B2*

In Australia: Please write to *Penguin Books Australia Ltd, P.O. Box 257, Ringwood, Victoria 3134*

In New Zealand: Please write to *Penguin Books (NZ) Ltd, Private Bag 102902, North Shore Mail Centre, Auckland 10*

In India: Please write to *Penguin Books India Pvt Ltd, 706 Eros Apartments, 56 Nehru Place, New Delhi 110 019*

In the Netherlands: Please write to *Penguin Books Netherlands bv, Postbus 3507, NL-1001 AH Amsterdam*

In Germany: Please write to *Penguin Books Deutschland GmbH, Metzlerstrasse 26, 60594 Frankfurt am Main*

In Spain: Please write to *Penguin Books S. A., Bravo Murillo 19, 1° B, 28015 Madrid*

In Italy: Please write to *Penguin Italia s.r.l., Via Felice Casati 20, I-20124 Milano*

In France: Please write to *Penguin France S. A., 17 rue Lejeune, F–31000 Toulouse*

In Japan: Please write to *Penguin Books Japan, Ishikiribashi Building, 2–5–4, Suido, Bunkyo-ku, Tokyo 112*

In Greece: Please write to *Penguin Hellas Ltd, Dimocritou 3, GR–106 71 Athens*

In South Africa: Please write to *Longman Penguin Southern Africa (Pty) Ltd, Private Bag X08, Bertsham 2013*